The Wisdom of the Witches
Book 3 - Witch Wisdom Series
By Sarah Lewin © 2024

---

1. http://www.sarahlewin.com

This book is dedicated to:
Authors who inspire a sense of mischief, magic, and mystery
My teachers, parents, and author friends
My four beautiful grown-up children and my amazingly patient husband
And my friends who I have met along my journey
I couldn't have written this without you

Chapter One

Stella

One day. Couldn't the universe have given them longer to celebrate Stella's return before sending another bombshell? The coven wasn't asking for much, but a few days to relax, rest, laugh, eat, and drink would be nice.

Up until six months ago, Stella, in her late thirties, single mother of four grown-ups, some of whom spoke to her, two who didn't, lived in a large town in Australia. An average, normal person. Until she found a portal in the bottom of the backyard in the property she rented. Instead of the high metal colourbond fence she expected to see as she chased a flash of movement through the prickly fruit trees, she'd found herself in an alleyway in medieval Scotland. She never figured out what had coerced her outside, though likely a fairy or a sprite, had been sent to help as her magic awakened.

"It feels like we've known you forever." Maisie hugged Stella for the fourth time in as many hours. Stella wasn't normally comfortable with such affection, but she shared her new friend's relief to have banished the evil that threatened to steal magic from this realm and power from the modern world. "It's only been a few months and for some of that you were kidnapped." Maisie's hair blonde hair hung loose around her face. The emotional one of the three friends, it worried her that Stella put herself in danger far too often.

Stella tugged her long brown hair back into a ponytail, her preferred way of wearing her hair. Brigid's tavern felt like home, as much as her little cottage back in modern Australia, maybe more so. The scent of wood, mixed with mead, sweet meats and baked bread, the bustle and chatter of the customers, it hadn't taken long for Stella to consider this her second home. The three women bonded immediately, over a common goal – to save their realm from evil. Brigid, with her flaming red hair, as bold as Maisie was timid. Both fiercely loyal to each other, their home and now Stella, the newcomer from the other side of the world. Missing her children, all the time, since they were torn away far too early for her to be prepared for the empty nest, the bond she shared with these two was quite literally magic.

"Oh, come on!" Brigid, her red hair piled up in a messy bun, pretended to frown at her oldest friend. "It's not like Stella's helpless. She's managed to save her world and our realm, again, after discovering her magic a few months ago." She handed her friends a tankard each. Maisie's contained mead as to be expected in the tavern Brigid owned and ran in the medieval market town in southwest Scotland. Stella's contained coffee, a magic concoction Brigid prepared especially for Stella, who'd been sober for a while now.

Sipping the strange dark brew, Stella tried not to regret her addictive behaviour, drinking too much alcohol – wine, and spirits, and smoking, once her children decided to take their fathers side, and move in with him. She'd gone off the rails, when the smarter thing to do would've been to get sober and get her kids back. Regret won't change the past. She shook her head, clearing the melancholy away.

"When's the next celebration?" Stella was bummed at missing the last moon festival. "I still have so much to learn from you. I may be magic, but having only just discovered my abilities, I'm looking forward to fully immersing in everything here."

"It'll be good to have life get back to normal." Brigid agreed. "For everyone. So many people were asking about you and when you'd return and open your apothecary."

"That's been on my mind too. Tomorrow morning I'll see what needs to be done to set it right. It feels like I've been away for such a long time." Stella sipped from her tankard. The coffee was stronger, thicker compared to the modern world. It didn't give her a headache, no matter how much she drank. She suspected it may contain a drop of mead or alcohol of some kind. In this realm spirits and wine didn't affect her the way it did in the world where she grew up. The last thing she wanted was to fall victim to any more addictions.

"We shut the door and left the mess. I couldn't face cleaning up." Two small tears formed in Maisie's eyes, as she remembered the last time she'd ventured into Stella's shop.

Their plan, to use the spirit of a powerful ancestor to banish a malevolent coven succeeded, but it could've ended badly. Hecate, a powerful witch in Stella's family tree, had channelled through her, coming to their aid to banish a coven of malevolent witches from the realms. Led by Cain, an evil witch who'd spent his entire life trying to steal everyone's magic in this realm, and the power and wealth from Stella's world, The Coven, originally named *The Mark of the Thirteen*, were formidable opponents. With the aid of her coven, Hecate and some other witches, Stella managed to defeat him twice.

"Do you still feel her?" Brigid asked.

"It's only been a day or so." Stella mused. "Maybe Hecate makes herself known when there's danger? I'm happy to be spending time with you both. I'll let you know if she returns." She promised, seeing the worried look on Maisie's face. "When are we catching up with Luna and the others?"

"Tomorrow evening, if they can make it." Brigid passed another tray of cheese and fruits to Stella. "They're in the middle of preparations for the equinox."

"One minute I think I've been here forever, then you say words like equinox, and I'm reminded how much I don't remember or know about life here." Stella sighed as she passed the platter around to the patrons enjoying an evening drink or two.

The tavern stayed open late most nights, tonight, even later than normal. None of Brigid's customers minded that the three women lost track of time. If her door was unlocked, customers would wander in for mead, ales and sustenance. Neither Stella nor Maisie minded helping, pleased to be spending time together without having to be worried that evil was prowling about. None of them noticed the hooded figure lurking outside. There was no need for the patrons to mention the being, it wasn't an unusual sight. People wore cloaks and hoods as protection against the bitter cold.

Stella's senses tingled. Sparks of electrical energy shot through her arms. She caught the little flashes as they left her fingertips, directing them away from the customers. She glanced around, wondering who'd set off her intuition.

Beware

The ominous warning from Hecate, or one of her other spirit guides didn't surprise her. She was getting used to these messages. The voices, one of the early manifestations of her magic, were as much of her life as her friends, and her children. Along with the time slips, portals, and her abilities, she learnt not to be afraid of them anymore. Heeding the voice, Stella's eyes swept around the room. Did she recognise the patrons, nursing their drinks? Were they innocent customers of the tavern or something more sinister? Stella chuckled to herself; she was being ridiculous. Brigid or Maisie would know if any of the customers posed a threat. Still, the word lingered, like an acrid smell, or elusive words to a song.

"Let's sit. You look like you need some food." Brigid sat a plate piled with sweet breads on the table in front of Stella. The closest booth to the larder, was fast becoming their regular table. From here Stella could see the whole room. The group of younger males dressed in long brown robes, their long hair braids hung loosely along their back, decided to blast out a song, as the mead loosened their vocal cords. The only threat there to the ear drums of the other patrons. A couple of older men, bleary eyed, staring into their tankards, seemed harmless. One of them muttered to himself as the minutes ticked by. Stella felt her friends' eyes on her as she contemplated the clientele. She bit into a piece of sweet bread. Doughy, but tough, chewy it reminded Stella of the damper she'd made in girl guides. She wished she could introduce her friends to some of the foods available in the modern age. This stuff was solid enough to knock someone out, if she aimed properly. She'd never let her new friends know that she didn't enjoy the foods they prepared for their feasts.

"Delicious as always, and exactly what I needed. I must've been hungrier than I realised." She raised her tankard. "Thank you, for being awesome friends. A few minutes ago, my intuition warned me to be aware, I'm not sure what is wrong, but no one here appears to be a threat. Still, we must be mindful, tonight, and always. I imagine the *Mark of the Thirteen*, or whatever the coven calls themselves, aren't pleased we ended their plans for world domination. Kai's warned us the coven numbers have grown from the original thirteen families."

"Will she be back?" Brigid asked, as she wiped out some empty tankards with the cloth she kept behind the bar.

"Maybe one day. She's her own coven and her own destiny to deal with." Stella knew a little of Kai's history and was certain their paths would cross again. "She originally escaped the castle and her obligations to her ancestral coven, as a teenager. To save her friends and the children they rescued, Kai returned to the castle and pretended to work with her evil cousin." Kai, Cain's cousin by birth, chose to spend her life saving children in need. Although Cain forced Kai to spy on Stella, they'd worked together to banish him. "I trust her." Stella continued. "I know Luna has her doubts, and I understand that, but I've no doubt Kai would help us again, if we needed her to."

Brigid nodded. "Luna will come around; she's been hurt so much she doesn't trust anyone. It took a while for her to realise you weren't evil. Losing her children while she fought to save the folk in this realm from The Coven, I understand how that could make you suspicious of everyone."

"Considering everything that's happened to her, I don't blame her for being sceptical." Stella agreed. "It's my normal line of defence, when I meet people. With you guys, I felt like I'd found a missing piece. I guess that's how Luna feels with Cahterine and Tizzie."

"The bond shared between members of a coven is something we can only understand once part of a coven." Brigid said, as she piled the empty platters on the end of the bar.

Maisie collected tankards left on the tables as patrons left, swiping clean the table tops with the edge of her robes. Stella wasn't yet used to the layers of clothing worn in this realm, but she appreciated the warmth they offered. "We could stay here tonight." Maisie ventured, the thought of what Cain and his malevolent coven were capable of, scared her. "In case there's a threat. Tomorrow we can go to the apothecary together."

"What about your customers? They'll expect to buy new clothes and fabrics, as they prepare for the festivities and the warmer weather." Brigid said sternly. Maisie's dress and fabric shop was popular amongst the locals and travellers from further away, her fabrics vibrant and rich in colour and texture. The dresses reminded Stella of those princesses wore in the stories of her childhood. Were the clothes modelled on those fairy tales? Or were the fairy tales retelling of life here in this realm? Did magical creatures create the gowns? The gowns and robes didn't seem practical, she had a habit of tripping over long skirts. Stella preferred to wear jeans or leggings.

"Once we're certain there's no evil waiting for her, I'll go to work, as long as we can meet here after work." Maisie reached into the large wooden box under the bench seat against the back wall. She lifted out a pile of blankets, depositing them on the wooden bench seats at the back of the tavern.

"Out ye go, here's some food to tide you over. We'll be open early tomorrow, as you know. No, you can't sleep here too." Brigid gently ushered the old codgers out. The young ones, arms around each other, their singing heard as they danced arm in arm along the road to their rooms. "They've rooms to go to, and blankets too, we organised that before the cold hit, we didn't want our customers freezing to death." Brigid explained, as the oldies grumbled, but grudgingly allowed the tavern owner to shoo them out the door.

A yawn escaped; Stella couldn't help it. The warmth of the rough wooden bench, the thick homemade blanket and the blazing fire; it was comfortable. Stella yawned again. Her friends already snuggled in their spots. She slid her feet and legs along the length of the bench, allowing her head to rest on the padded cushion. Hand woven, she recognised the weave as something very old, an antique she'd seen in a museum once, a long time ago. In this realm these were new, hand stitched by one of the travellers who imported the fabric from the orient. "Good night." She muttered to her friends who were breathing evenly, exhausted after the craziness of the last few days. It felt good to be back amongst friends.

Stella and her coven dozed, no one noticed the figure outside, or heard him try the lock. The ancient protection spell, cast years before Stella's arrival, kept them safe. For now.

Chapter Two

S tella

"We can't carry on mistrusting everyone new who comes in looking for food or drink." Brigid scolded Maisie, as she peered through the window at the early morning throng of people heading to the market. "We can't possibly know everyone by name. What about the travellers? Our market town is a place that draws them to sell their wares on their way to and from the other realms." Stella listened in silence, enjoying being back with her friends.

"Fine." Maisie harrumphed as she unlocked the door and held it open for the early morning customers on their way to the market or to ports further away. Three of the older men that Stella recognised from the previous day, tipped their hats to Maisie as they walked past.

"The rumours were right, she returns." A tall male boomed in a loud voice. With a bow and a flourish, he swung the door open wide. "Welcome back." He turned to Brigid "I expected to see the tavern bustling, and a feast in honour of her return. The news has spread far and wide amongst the realms." Logan, a distant cousin of Brigid's whom Stella met the year before, grinned, his brown eyes full of mischief. His thick dark hair was longer than Stella remembered.

"Oh, hush you! Where were you yesterday? A feast like you've never seen, and you were a day late." Brigid made to whip him with her cleaning cloth. "Help yourself to the food and drink, you know where it all is." Brigid waved her arms in the general direction of the bar area.

"Some sweetmeats to fortify me for the day ahead would be wonderful." His dark eyes danced, knowing how easy it was to stir up his cousin. He grabbed a piece off the platter.

A cold air followed Logan into the tavern. Stella shivered and wrapped her coat tightly around her shoulders. While not of this world, her purple coat, which she'd discovered at the back of her wardrobe in her world contained a magic from this world. Since finding it, the pockets often revealed exactly what she required in any given tricky situation. It hung loosely but not too much to trip her up or restrict movements. It kept her warm when she needed it, she rarely wandered around without it, since stumbling across it a few months ago. Handmade, the embroidery and dainty stitches, not quite patchwork, of a material she seen at the stalls at the market.

A movement at the door, she noticed a shadow of a hooded figure standing just outside the tavern, staring at them. His eyes dark, he was tall and ominous. She felt, rather than saw the evil in his aura. Before she could alert the others, Logan spoke again.

"Three cheers for Stella." Logan raised the tankard Brigid handed to him. "Sorry I missed your return. You discovered your magic powers, less than a year ago. In that time, you stumbled across our tavern, and helped save the world from evil, not once, but twice." A rowdy cheer chorused from the early morning customers, and a clinking of tankards. "This time, try not to lose her again," Logan grinned cheekily.

Maisie who was handing around trays of sweet breads and assorted cuts of meat, swiped at him with her hand.

"It was hardly Brigid and Maisie's fault." Stella protested. "If I'd listened to them, I'd have been more careful and not put myself in a position where I could be kidnapped. Did you notice anything odd outside, before you entered?"

"Nope. Nothing unusual. Except I'm missing my friends who are a day away, due to meet me here tomorrow. Angus and Blair stayed at the harbour an extra day, to trade with the ship due in from the orient. I've business in the next town, so I left earlier. Why do you ask?" Logan shoved a piece of cheese into his mouth, not waiting for Stella's response.

"I thought I noticed something unusual. It's probably my overactive imagination." Stella spoke, more to herself than the others. After all, what evil would be lurking on the other side of the door? With Kai's help she'd banished the evil from this realm, and if the stories were true, it'd be at least twenty-seven years before the next round of evil was due to return.

A sense of contentment and peace filled her heart. Her children were halfway across the world and several centuries away. She'd plans to visit them in a couple of months. The four of them travelling and working overseas together, she held out hope that the younger two would convince the older two to at least say hello. Stella refused to let regret and loss get to her here in this magical realm. While her kitten was growing up without her, the neighbour loved Puddles almost as much as she did. No need for her to worry about him or the house she'd inherited from a friend. She loved it here, with Maisie and Brigid, her coven and the opportunity to learn how to use her powers. Everything as it should be for now. No more trouble or danger.

"Can anyone smell smoke?" Maisie sniffed the air as one of the regulars left the door open on their way to work at the markets down the road.

"Probably a household trying to keep warm." Brigid polished the empty tankards and hung each one up ready for its next use. "Spring mornings there's still a chill in the air."

Stella wasn't sure. Still on high alert after her recent kidnapping and her battle to save the world. "Maybe one of us should go and check it out?" she ventured, putting her tankard on the table.

"You'll do no such thing." Exclaimed Maisie. "If there's something wrong, we'll know soon enough. Let someone else take care of it. Drink up and eat something too. I'm not sure that you ate properly while you were away."

"The city of Brisbane, in the present day, is not some desolate desert or prison." Stella laughed. "We eat fairly well in Australia in 2024." She drank from the tankard Brigid made for her. The bitter taste, with a little fortifying spirit was the perfect morning drink. "One day I'll tell you about some of the foods and drinks available, or better still, maybe one day you'll come and visit our world."

"Still, I'd like to make sure you're okay, now you're back. You aren't planning on leaving again?" Maisie fussed around, reminding Stella of a mother hen making sure her chicks were out of harm's way.

Stella drained the rest of her drink. She was eager to get to work. The last time she'd been in her store, she'd left it a little messy. "I wasn't planning on it last time, that's why it's called kidnapping. I'm keen to set up my apothecary and learn some more magic. Spend some time with you and Brigid. Then I'm going to visit my kids."

Before Maisie could complain about Stella's plans, the door slammed open, and Angus and Blair marched in. Neither as tall as Logan, Blair's long sandy hair was tied in a pigtail, Angus's hung loose around his face, reminding Stella of a shaggy dog. The smell of smoke hung heavy in the air. Voices outside echoed, though Stella couldn't make out any words, the sense of panic conveyed through the energy rippling past the open door.

"Careful of the door." Brigid admonished them. "Not that the likes of you'd damage it, it's far too heavy. What if someone was behind it when you flung it open/"

"There's a fire at the market. It's a mess." The youngest of Logan's coven glanced at Brigid, apprehension showing on his young face. "Not ignoring you, but we need to help them."

With a glance at Brigid that said *not again*, and a sinking feeling in the pit of her stomach, Stella followed the others out the door.

"Wait for us," Maisie yelled. Stella heard footsteps, and the thud of the tavern door being shut, but didn't turn back. Adrenalin propelling her forward. Her heart thumping loudly, with so many people yelling out for loved ones, she doubted anyone could hear it. She felt the rough rope end of a sturdy wooden bucket shoved into her hand. She turned to see Maisie and Brigid, each holding a bucket, ready to help extinguish the fire.

Before discovering the portal at the bottom of her garden, an ordinary single mother, and teacher, never thought she find herself helping to extinguish a blaze in a medieval town in Scotland. Dumfries, a market town since the twelfth century, a place where ordinary and magical people worked hand in hand, side by side. Like a page from a book, or a scene from a movie, traders set up permanent and temporary stalls, in front of the taverns, public houses and accommodation. Other travellers, Stella knew them as gypsies, offered more exotic wares from faraway places.

Stella experienced the sensation she'd been here before. Did she believe in reincarnation? Probably, given the recent history. Through the smoke and flames, she saw the fabric and lace, the spices and herbs from the orient and the leatherwork, bone work and other wares. Edible delicacies, breads, sweet biscuits, like muffins, exotic fruits and pieces of meat too exotic for Stella to even guess at their origin. The bittersweet pungent mix of aromas assaulted her senses. Her eyes stung, her stomach lurched, her energy on alert for danger, impossible to find in the anxiety and upset of those gathered in the square.

People crowded around the water fountain, filling buckets. Bystanders formed a line, passing the wooden buckets along to merchants closer to where the flames were licking the wagons of breads, sweetmeats and leatherwork. The pungent aroma of burning animal fat turned Stella's stomach inside out. She cringed, the hissing noise as the water reached the fire as disturbing as the lingering stench threatening to make her lose the contents of her stomach. She heaved, determined not to add to the chaos. The flames danced around and grew a little higher, teasing those who were trying their best to save the town.

"Don't let it spread to the buildings." Called a frantic voice from the back of the crowd. "My mother's room is upstairs, over there." Heads turned towards the voice, craning their necks to see where she was pointing.

By the time Stella and her coven filled their buckets, she knew she must do something more. Worried the sparks that flew from her fingers when her magic intensified, might make the fires worse, she focused on the water in the buckets. In her mind's eye, the water increased until it became a river, washing over the fire, extinguishing it, but leaving little damage in its wake. Her body tingled with the now familiar strength as her magic energy wove the story in her vision.

A gasp from the crowd startled Stella. As if waking from a trance she caught her breath as she surveyed the scene in front of her. Had she done that? Flames no longer licked up the sides of the buildings. As if someone laid a damp blanket over the fire, only a few wisps of smoke and some charred and sooty produce remained as evidence of the flames.

A cheer emanated from behind her. Stella turned to see Logan, Blair, and Angus fist pumping and clapping. The rest of the crowd copied them. The group who'd been frozen in place seconds before were congratulating each other on saving the town from inevitable destruction. With a makeshift ladder leaning against a building, a group of younger men assisted an old woman to safety.

"How did you do that?" Brigid's voice whispered in Stella's ear.

"I've no idea. I simply pictured the water turning into a river, putting out the fire but not causing water damage. Maybe Hecate guided my magic?"

"I think the water came from you, your power, not hers. Hers feels different, there's a series of strong and powerful ancients behind her. Your strength is tempered with kindness, although your magic is becoming more powerful. We haven't seen a magic like yours in this realm for many years." She put her hands on her hips and frowned. "I don't understand why everyone thinks it was a team effort." Stella's eyes followed Maisie's gaze. Those in the square were patting each other on the back, grinning and acting like their footy team won the grand finale.

"It's called misdirection I think." Stella said quietly, head spinning at what she'd achieved. "I don't mind if others want to celebrate, it takes the limelight off me. We're lucky the fire died before it caused more damage, or injury."

Logan bounced up behind them. "Brigid, how about you open the tavern and pour us a steadying mead. It'll take a while to clean up this mess. A fortifying drink beforehand is exactly what's needed." He placed his hands out in front, in a pleading motion. "I'll even help handing out the food."

An air of agitation permeated the market square. Not everyone would want a steadying mead but would instead prefer to make necessary repairs to stalls and salvage what stock wasn't irreparably damaged. "So generous of you." Brigid eyed him sarcastically. "Come on then, let the stallholders know we're providing a drink and some food for those who want it. Promise you'll return to help set the market right again."

"I'll bring some food back to the stall holders who don't want to leave." Maisie bit her lip, her eyes welled with tears as she surveyed the mess around them. The damage was mostly superficial, but it'd still take a day or two to clear away the soot, the charred goods and make the necessary repairs to some of the stalls. Thankfully there didn't appear to be much structural damage to the buildings around the square.

STELLA AND HER FRIENDS were too busy to notice the tall stranger, dressed in dark robes, his hood obscuring his face. His energy was dark, muted. He observed the mess with a wry smile. He'd not directly caused the fire, though he'd convinced a street urchin to start it. Told him it'd keep him and his sister warm. A diversion more than a malicious attempt to burn down the market, if that had been his desire, nothing could have stopped him. It afforded him the opportunity to observe Stella's skills first hand. There was more to her than he'd given her credit for. Shame he wouldn't be able to turn her. The pure goodness oozed from her, not an ounce of evil in that one. Pity, they would've made a powerful team. He stepped back, melting into the shadows as the three women passed by.

"MY APOTHECARY IS NOWHERE near the marketplace. There's no fire smouldering away, or any other hidden danger." Stella reassured Maisie, who looked doubtful. They could still hear the marketplace from outside Stella's shop, as people helped the traders repair their stalls and save what items they could.

They turned, hearing footsteps as Brigid caught up with them. "Logan and his friends are manning the tavern, handing out the food and drink. A couple of travellers offered their wagons to remove any rubbish to the outskirts of town. Logan promised me he'll make sure they're all fed, and not drink too much until it's all done."

Stella unlocked the door to her apothecary. The smell of the last spells they'd cast, the herbs used hit her as an invisible wave of energy escaped through the door. "It'll take ages to clean this up. I think we should stay and help." Maisie pointed to the upturned bottles of herbs, and the books strewn on the floor, under Stella's work bench. With everyone's focus on whether they'd succeeded in banishing the evil forces, no one thought to tidy up the apothecary. It wasn't high up on Maisie or Brigid's priorities, they'd been more worried about their friend. The fear Maisie felt leaving her friend the last time crept back in. "You need us to stay and burn some sage. It's too big a job to do by yourself."

"Nonsense, I'll get this sorted in time to meet you back at the tavern for lunch. You promised you'd try not to worry. Your clients will be wondering where you are." Stella knew she wouldn't be able to convince her friend that nothing would happen, if she stayed at the apothecary by herself, still she tried.

Maisie tried to protest as Brigid took her by the hand and led her away to her dress shop on the other side of the tavern. "Maisie, you promised." Brigid said firmly. "I'm going to make sure there's enough food in our larder, that the boys haven't eaten and drunk the tavern empty. You need to tend to your customers too."

It's not so bad. Stella told herself. *A few hours here and I'll be ready for customers.*

The little store, an apothecary years before Stella stumbled across it at the end of last year, stood alone and abandoned at the end of the row of shops down a side street from the market square, waiting for its next owner. It's black stone façade and black wooden door with little glass window instantly drew Stella in. The walls lined with shelves that held many jars and old books so thick with dust that she sneezed for the first few days, until the dust resettled on the floor to be swept out the door. The thick wooden shelves, lining two of the walls, held the energy of the tree from whom they were created. Stella hadn't yet worked out how the shelves sat on the stone walls, but they were anchored tight. A low bench ran along the third wall, a place to sleep for the previous occupant, possibly or for healing clients. Glass and metal lanterns with large wax candles hung on each wall. Their eerie glow didn't provide a lot of light to work by, Stella preferred to leave the door open, to encourage what light there was to enter.

Remembering to sage the shop, her fingers ran along the jars, *Mullein, Wormwood, Borage, Feverfew, Pennyroyal, Mugwort, Patchouli, Anise.* Was there an order to the way in which they were stored? By ailment maybe, or whether root, leaf or seed? Stella made a note to rearrange the herbs in alphabetical order the first chance she could. Easier to locate each one, at least until she became confident with the stock and their uses. With the jar of sage in her hand, she sprinkled some in the doorway, and around the walls. That would have to do. *Positive energy only please.* She added, aloud, remembering that setting the intention was as important as the action.

Stella arranged the books on the shelf on the opposite side of the store to the potions and herbs. She looked forward to the opportunity to sit and read through them one day soon, now that evil no longer threatened the realm, there'd be time. Stella's brain never stopped, keen to learn as much as she could, as quickly and possible. Her intuition and magic grew, the more she used her powers. She touched the leather cover of the *Book of Spells.* The book mysteriously arrived in her home in Australia, and somehow followed her wherever she found herself. She discovered it in the flat when she was separated from her coven, with new pages she hadn't seen before. Could this have been Hecates book? It belonged to her now, the warmth beneath her palms as she handled the book told her that.

Maybe somewhere in the book, or in one of the books she'd returned to the shelf, was a list of the magical uses for the herbs on her shelf. That would be handy, seeing as she wasn't sure what to recommend to customers. When she'd chosen the herbs to rid the realm of the malevolent coven, her intuition, entwined with Hecate's knowledge provided the answers. Stella shook her head. Overthinking things, a tendency of hers, never solved anything. She placed the last of the opaque jars back on the shelf. Who'd written the labels? Faded parchment, the herb names scratched on in a sharp black ink. Cursive writing, she could make out most of the words.

A couple of the travellers she'd spoken to, who regularly joined the market on a Friday were more than happy to bring specialist herbs, runes, and potions with them, for Stella to stock in her apothecary. They specialised in difficult to find items and made their own concoctions, items would be useful to her in her shop. After a few weeks, she'd have the best stocked herbal healing shop this side of the town. "I know I've a list of my stock here somewhere." She muttered, flipping over all the books in the shelf looking for the list she remembered writing when she first set up.

Luna's apothecary, on the other side of the town, contained an extensive range of products, to ease all ailments and stocked the most sought-after spell ingredients. Luna taught her which products were popular and those necessary for the most used spells. Where did she put that list? Stella slid her hand into the pocket of her coat, maybe she'd put it there. She'd found it in the back of her cupboard a few months ago - the coat had a habit of manifesting exactly what she needed at the right time. From crystals, directions to a portal or herbs to close all the portals, and this time it didn't disappoint. She pulled out the list of herbs she'd written a few weeks ago, missing her laptop, her hand ached by the time she'd completed the work. Someone, Stella, never questioned the origins of her coat and the gifts it provided, had added to the list - information on each herb, suggesting how best to use them

THE HOODED FIGURE STOOD outside her door, his face pressed against the glass, eyes watching Stella as she tidied her space. She swung around, feeling his eyes boring into the back of her head. He flinched and drew back from the open door, bumping it.

Her spider senses on high alert, Stella moved quickly to the door and checked outside. A tall figure, dressed in dark robes that dragged along the ground, disappeared around the corner at the end of the alley. As she turned back to re-enter her store, the sharp smell of peppermint permeated the air around her. The room in front of her, wasn't her cute little store, but a huge room, full of rows of bunks, each with a thin animal hair blanket as a mattress. More than a dozen children ran around the room, chasing each other, laughing as they fell over the black cat that wrapped itself around their ankles, causing them to fall to the ground giggling.

"Enough of that!" A tall man barely out of his teens, yelled with such authority that everyone froze. Even the cat. "It's time for chores, then lessons, then more chores. Fun is for good boys and girls who do as they are told."

"Yes master." Chorused the children.

He clapped his hands twice firmly. The noise rang out, Stella flinched, her ears pierced by the awful noise. What creature could make his hand clapping sound like a shrill whistle? Her heart ached for the little ones. Where were their parents?

"Fred Bell! You must set an example for the others. Laundry, now! Annette! Take the girls and start the meals. The rest of you, you know what to do." The figure glided out of sight. Stella watched as the older children led the others away. The image faded and she found herself at the door of her apothecary.

She'd visited that school before, in another lifetime. Intuition told her those children had parents, so it wasn't an orphanage. Stolen from their families and made to work. Hecates memories, so entwined with hers; the boarding house she'd visited part of the school where they were trained in the way of The Coven. The words and memories tumbled quickly before she could catch them. Hecate showed her the past for a reason. Was the figure lurking outside the figure yelling at the children? How long ago? Where were they now?

A little black spider, dangling in front of her eyes distracted her. Busily weaving a strong thread from the ceiling, to strengthen his web. Delicate, intricate, yet strong enough to catch and keep prey.

"Not my children." She told her new friend. "They're safe and sound in the UK, in my time." Her head throbbed at the thought that something like that could happen to her children, to any children. "I haven't spoken to them for a few days, but they're together, looking after each other." The scene she'd witnessed, felt like it occurred a long time ago. Had Kai's passion for rescuing stolen children originated there? Were those children friends of hers?

What was the connection between the scene and the figure who hurried down the road? "If I hadn't just helped in banishing the malevolent coven, I'd think they were still lurking, hiding in the shadows, taking innocents and indoctrinating them in the ways of the coven." As soon as the words left her mouth, she knew them to be true. Hecate's vision a warning that evil still lurked in the shadows. Her energy throbbed, the fuzziness of it rippled around her body. The spider's eyes grew wide, and he scrambled back up to the top of his web.

"There's something more." A horrible realisation dawned. "Children, stolen long ago. Oh my goodness. Luna!"

Chapter Three

L una
    Not far away, in a forest on the edge of the market town, Luna rummaged through the shelves in her apothecary. Impatiently, she wound her long grey hair up into a messy bun, capturing the wispy hair with a few hairpins and butterfly clips she found buried deep in the pocket of her worn purple cardigan.

"It's easier to see, with my hair out of the way." She muttered to the empty room. "I know it's here somewhere."

She turned her head, as a small black cat ran in through the open door.

"Ah Spider, there you are." The once stray and homeless orphan cat rubbed against Luna's legs. "Have you seen my *Book of Spells*? I didn't think I put it away on a shelf, but I can't find it anywhere."

Spider, named because the crone had to disentangle her from a large orb spider web, nudged the large wicker basket under the heavy wooden work bench. Luna reached in, her hand warming as she plucked her beloved book from its hiding place.

"I remember now, I put a protection spell on the basket after all the goings on with Stella and The Coven. I didn't want my book to fall into the wrong hands. It's not exactly a secure room." The older witch looked around the workshop that doubled as an apothecary. The locals on this side of the market town, the older townsfolk, frequented Luna's place to buy herbs, hard to find ingredients, and to learn how to create the more complex spells. Her shop less commercial and more haphazard, originally and still for the most part, a little cottage, on the very edge of this side of Dumfries, not far from *Catherine's Inn* and *Tizzie's Fabulous Fabric and Clothing Shop*. Shelves lined two walls, and jars of herbs, potions and lotions lay on most spaces, shelves crammed with seed pods, rocks, leaves and other items she'd collected over the years. Her home for as long as she chose it.

"The problem with having two homes, as lucky as that is for a crone like me, is that I can never find what I'm looking for. It's in one place or another. Normally the other." The witch thumbed through the book, temporarily forgetting why she searched for it in the first place. She admired the drawings. "Did I draw that? Or someone else?" She wondered aloud.

Like Stella, Luna lived in this world and the modern one, through several centuries and halfway around the world. "I'm so glad I returned, even though I didn't want to at first." She crooned, picking up Spider. The cat let her friend pat her, though there were mice to sniff out. "I did miss Catherine and Tizzie when I lived there." The coven of old crones mirrored the younger ones, for reasons not yet clear to anyone.

"I was content in my little cottage in the bush in Queensland. With my magpie and my kitten. Now I don't want to leave here. It's like I'm torn in two." Luna told her familiar, in medieval Scotland which was her other home. Some days she couldn't remember which came first, the connection with both so strong. The lines blurred, as did the memories of her lives and the people she'd loved and lost.

The heat of her tears stung her eyes. She squeezed them shut tight, trying to wash away the memory of the last time her life was torn apart. "As a mother, I'm not meant to lose my children before they grow." Spider tried to wipe the tears away with her coarse tongue, as they spilt down Luna's face. So gentle, she patted her witch with her paws, and without claws, as familiars can do, when caring for their human.

The stabbing pain that burned her heart when she thought of Freddie, Annie, Lizzie, and Katie caused her to drop the cat. Spider, used to the crone's clumsiness, prepared herself, landing elegantly on her feet.

You didn't lose them, they were taken from you, because you chose to help save people.

Sometimes the witch couldn't distinguish between her thoughts and her spirit guides. Today it didn't matter. The loss of her children, always her fault in her heart and mind, though their father and evil forces were behind it. She could have chosen a different path. Refused to help, even though her powers drew her into battle.

There's no time for regret.

The voice persisted.

This is your journey. They have theirs.

"Yes, they do." Luna whispered. "But why can't their journey and mine be connected and peaceful?"

She'd searched for her children, after helping banish the malevolent coven, for twenty-seven years, or maybe longer. Time passes quickly some days and painfully slow on others. Such a long time ago, they'd disappeared, without a trace. So had their father, he who'd threatened to take them far away, so she'd never be able to connect with them or find them ever. She'd misread his threat, as another empty promise. She'd underestimated his ability to follow through on his bully whisperings. He didn't have powers, did he? Oh, my goodness, that was too much to bear thinking about. Bad enough her powers cost her the children.

After the war, her coven, Catherine and Tizzie, helped her search. Others from this realm and back in the other world, where magic was the stuff of fairy tales and books, many tried to locate her missing bairns. Their father must've taken them, changed their names and they grew up happy, and well adjusted, albeit without their mother. That was the only scenario she could come up with, as to why she'd not been able to find a clue or a hint of where they may be. As long as they were safe, and happy. Painful beyond compare, but she could handle that thought.

"I'm never giving up, even though each day is a day further since I last saw them. Instead of the babies I remember they're all grown." Would her children have inherited any of her powers?

She thumbed through the well-worn sepia parchment pages of her hand made book. A protection spell for her children. A simple spell, more love than protection, though a mother's love was the fiercest protection spell there is.

A rose quartz, a sprig of lavender, and a lot of love.

Love for my children and a little self-love too.

Little by little.

Healing.

THE HOODED FIGURE, in the long dark robe watched, hidden, out of sight. Spider tried to turn her crone's attention to the doorway, but Luna, too intense and lost in her dreams to notice. Family loss consumed her every full moon, some months worse than others. There'd be time to focus her witch to the threat lurking outside the door. Tomorrow.

Deep in the recess of her brain, the crone tried to remember. There was a clue, forever out of reach, hidden tantalizingly off the tip of her tongue. "Close my eyes, close my eyes." She muttered. "Activate my mind's eye, my third eye, though I have only two." Luna touched the middle of her forehead. As she did, an image of a tattoo passed by her vision. She reached out her hand as if to catch it. The tattoo disappeared like shimmery gossamer threads. "My third eye, that sees things that others can't see, things that don't exist. Like that." She waved her finger at the inky tattoo of an eye in a witch's star that kept flashing in front of her eyes. "Stars in my eyes." There's something about that tattoo, she was meant to remember. Her arm fell to her side, as it eluded her again.

A mouse, curious at the mutterings of the old crone, poked her head out of her hole. She ran up the leg of the table to get a better look and knocked over a book balanced on the corner. The noise startled the witch. Luna jumped, dust flying around her as she grabbed the corner of one of the shelves to steady herself.

From her spot near the door, where she was ready to pounce, if the hooded figure tried to enter, Spider watched the mouse. The cat had absolutely no interest in chasing or eating the furry creature.

All thoughts of the tattoo forgotten; Luna brushed herself off. "What was I doing?" she asked no one in particular. "A cup of peppermint tea. Just the thing. Everything is better with tea." She scooped some water out of the pot that sat on the little black pot belly stove in the middle of the store. Opening the jar on the bench she shook out some peppermint leaves not bothering with the little strainer. She stared at the mug, willing the water to cool enough to drink it. Impatiently tapping on the worktop in a pattern from her life before her children disappeared. She traced an outline of an eye and a five-pointed star on the top of the workbench, repeating each stroke until the image was indelibly marked by the oil and the dust on the wood. As she drank her tea the tea leaves got stuck in her throat. Discarding the mug, the crone wandered to the shelf on the other side of her store, looking for something. The mouse peered into mug full of warm water and soggy leaves. The image on the table replicated in the mug. Spider swung the door shut, causing dust and sunbeams to fly up in the air. Whatever her crone was doing, it was important that the darkness lurking outside didn't see it.

Chapter Four

B roomhilda

This threat, sinister, insidious, it wafted in the air, the trees tossing it around, not wanting to hold the energy for any longer than they had to. An evil that wouldn't stay in its place, wouldn't stay banished. The thirst for magic, the hunger for power, contagious and spreading through the realm.

The fairy, the oldest magical being in this land, stood less than twenty centimetres tall. The most powerful magic creature saw the future and the past, not in clear pictures, but in colours, moods, auras, and energy. The ancient trees whispered to her. The fairies, elves, and other creatures passed on information, and communicated important messages to covens and other magical being throughout the realms. The messages being shown to her, in the aftermath of the last attempt at ridding the world of evil caused her more than a little concern.

"This is disturbing." She spoke aloud, in the forest, to the ancient tree, whose trunk sat as wide as an elephant's behind, its branches and roots stretched out, sending ancient energy and wisdom throughout this magical place. The magic of the ancient yew kept all who wandered by, safe. Malevolence couldn't penetrate this deep into the magic fairy glen. The river that ran through past the tree, started life as a brook in the mountain at the edge of Broomhilda's castle. Fairies tended the extensive gardens surrounding the castle. The harvests were given to those who needed food, or traded with wares from the elves, the pixies, sprites and others in the realm. The fairy glen proper, where the council of representatives, including Stella, met to discuss matters of urgency, was protected by ancient fae magic.

Broomhilda stopped and sniffed the sweet aroma of the daintiest daisy. A purple butterfly with frilly wings flew past. A dainty blue bird warbled, calling his mate to the tree with the bright red cherries.

"I hope I'm wrong." She told the butterfly as it landed on the flower next to her. "If our spell didn't work and the malevolence is still loose in our world we must act now. The longer we wait, the more out of balance our world becomes."

A little brown mouse, with a tail twice as long as his body scurried along the rocks on the edge of the stream. He looked at Broomhilda. She smiled and waved as he moved along, searching out some food for his family.

The tree swayed in the breeze and with the lyrical words uttered by Broomhilda, the fairy whose magic remained stronger than any other, even after so many years alive. "Balance. We must regain the balance."

There was no way around it, she had to let the others know.

"I DIDN'T WANT TO HAVE to call you all here so soon after Stella returned. I know you were looking forward to getting back to normal, a peaceful existence." Broomhilda's voice carried over the crowd gathered in the fairy glen, without the aid of a microphone. Small, but powerful, not one being on council challenged her role of leader. None were keen to take on the responsibility that went hand in hand with ensuring the safety of the realm.

The magic council consisted of representatives from each of the groups in the realm. Fairies, elves, sprites, gnomes, and people from the oldest magical families. Logan and his clan were the messengers who carried the council's message further than the edges of this realm. Luna, Stella and their respective covens embraced as they arrived and were now glued on Broomhilda's words.

"*The Mark of the Thirteen*, the malevolent coven that is many more than thirteen or thirteen times thirteen is growing. The hunger for power and knowledge is intoxicating for so many. I fear we need a new way of containing the threat. A new way, not merely banishing, or exiling them, which appears to be less permanent that we thought, but ridding The Coven from the realms once and for final."

A hush fell over the glen. Birds, insects and other creatures were silent. Not a leaf or a blade of grass rustled. Broomhilda felt the weight of the eyes of those present, eagerly waiting for her to tell them how she was going to solve this problem. Despite her age and wisdom, she wasn't prepared for this. There should've been a twenty-seven-year break from this level of war. Time to grow and consolidate and live freely and without fear. The cycle, the pattern broken; what other changes were subtly being woven into the realm?

Doubt and worry a heavy load on the fairy's shoulders, Stella sensed it. "It's not up to Broomhilda to solve this for us. Each of us belong on this council and have a role to play. We've tried to be fair. That hasn't worked. Why didn't the banishment work this time, what's changed? Is there another way? Who among us has firsthand knowledge of this coven and their ways? Who knows old magic?" As she finished her sentence, a voice in her head, Hecate, responded.

I do.

Luna stood beside Stella. "Together we can defeat them. Our ancestors have passed the knowledge onto us. We've fought this evil before. They grow stronger, and so do we." Like Stella, Luna discovered her abilities later in life, as a mum, and suffered insurmountable loss because of it. Words, phrases, knowledge, incantations, spells came to her from nowhere. Made her appear scatter brained, except to those like Stella and Broomhilda, who knew better. "We have books, words of wisdom, skills, spells and enchantments, the responsibility to solve this is ours, collectively."

Broomhilda drew herself up to her full height, nearly as tall as a carton of milk. "Our ancestors' books are buried somewhere, in the garden, at the back of the cupboard, under the sink, in the sock drawer. Find their books, evoke their protection spells, now if you know them, or when the tomes are in your possession." Broomhilda rose up to the height of one of the rose stems as it moved in search of sunlight. She stretched her tiny wings and flew to one of the lower branches of the yew. She held the gaze of as many of the council as she could, her voice strong, determined. "Keep in communication with your clan, through dreams and in person. There's an added safety in numbers."

"How long 'ave we got?" Yelled an elf named Punk. His shock of green hair stood straight up, making it difficult for him to wear a hat.

"I've been told Cain and his army of followers are reaching out to outsiders, recruiting them to their coven. The travellers, the traders, those who work by themselves, with no strong family ties. Loners, people on the fringes of society; they prey on the marginalised. Their army is growing in numbers, getting ready to take magic and power, by force if needed. Historically their interest has been in humans, not elves, fairies or other magical beings." Broomhilda flew closer to the group of elves at the back of the crowd, her voice took on a softer tone. "I can't be sure, but I don't think you're in any direct danger. We should still be careful, keep close to home, stay with your families. Humans don't expect us to get ourselves into danger to protect them. It's not our fight directly. Our magic is sacred, part of the very fabric of our world."

"That's true. Cain isn't after fae magic or elfin magic. He's scared of it. He's a coward and a bully. That's why he targeted children, initially and now those who are disgruntled with their lot in life." A woman with a shock of purple hair under a black hooded jumper stood up beside Stella.

"Kai!" Stella embraced her newest friend. "This is Kai." Stella spoke to the gathering. "Kai was born a member of the malevolent coven, Cain's her cousin. She ran away from the castle as a teenager and has spent the rest of her life rescuing children and working against the *Mark of the Thirteen*." She raised her voice, as the crowd started talking amongst themselves.

"How can we trust her? If she's one of them?" Punk yelled. A flurry of words, and a buzzing passed through the group. Even the birds and insects hummed and chirped, curious about the newcomer. A couple of mice scampered to get a closer look at Stella and Kai.

"I can understand your reticence." Broomhilda's voice cut into the conversations. "There's no need for concern. Kai helped Stella save us. Born into that coven, she chose a different path. One that respects all life, she works tirelessly to rescue children from The Coven." Perched above the crowd, her vantage point meant she could monitor the emotions of the crowd. All eyes turned towards Kai.

"I walked away from home when I turned fifteen. I've made it my life's work – rescuing children from their clutches. I returned last year, I let myself get captured, so I could keep my real coven and the children safe. My cousin will know by now that I'm not working with him anymore. Unless his ego is so inflated that he thinks I'm here to trick you and believe me his ego is that big." Kai shook her hood off so everyone could see her face.

"So how do we know we can trust you?" Luna asked curious, more than anything else. "You say your left the coven, but that you rejoined them for a few months, and that you've now left them again. How do we know what's true, that you're not here to spy on us?"

"I trust her." Stella spoke firmly. "She helped me, helped us, when she didn't have to. Her cousin tasked her to keep me from figuring out his plans. She could've stopped me using my magic, instead she helped me figure it all out and return here. It's not her fault we couldn't banish Cain and The Coven. We must've underestimated the extent of his power."

"Cain is malicious and spiteful, and the others are just as bad. They're greedy and don't care who gets hurt as long as their magic and power grow." Kai paused, running her hands through her hair. "None of them realise that once they succeed, he won't let anyone else share the spoils of war. His ego is his biggest failing. He'll doubt we can defeat him. If we can work together, collecting the spells of long ago, and learn from history, we'll win."

"I know it's asking a lot, but you can trust us." Stella added, wrapping her arm around her friend. You all gave me a chance and believed in me when I only just discovered my own power. You don't have to listen to me, but if you're willing to, find your families spell books. Ask your ancestors, find out how they defeated The Coven in the past and share the information amongst yourselves. Sharing knowledge with those you trust will help keep you safe."

Luna stood beside Stella and Kai. She glanced at them both, then turned to the wider group. "I don't know if I trust Kai yet, but I trust Stella. Years ago, my children were taken away from me when I chose to help rid the realm of this evil. The last couple of times we've tried, their evil is less affected and keeps growing. I'm willing to do whatever it takes to succeed this time. There must be a solution. One of your ancestors' books may hold the answer."

"What if we're willing to share with Broomhilda, but not anyone else?" Asked a fairy from the back of the room. He was dressed in blue and stood a little to one side.

Broomhilda flew over so she was hovering near the timid fairy. "Then your spell stays between you and me. I won't share it with anyone else. That's my promise to you, to each of you." Her voice grew in strength though her stature remained small.

Logan stuck his hand up. All eyes turned towards him. "Look, I don't know Kai, and I've only known Stella a short time. I've seen what Stella can do. Like Luna, she's been selfless in helping us save the realm. Sure, it didn't go according to plan, but we were missing something. Maybe Kai is what we were missing. I'm willing to trust Stella, and Kai and see how this plays out. Our numbers far outweigh Cain's currently." He fidgeted with the belt that hung loose around his shirt. "My friends and I'll go to the other realms and warn them about what's going on. The impact to the magic will be felt throughout the lands."

The oldest fairy moved over to the edge of the gathering and spoke to the group of fairies who were chattering softly amongst themselves. After a few moments of conversation in a fae language, the fairies flew away through the canopy of trees.

As if they'd been waiting in line, the elves trooped over to where Broomhilda stood away from the crowd. A few animated gruff voices could be heard, but in a language understood by elves and Broomhilda. After a short series of raise voices, and stamping of feet, the elves disappeared amongst the undergrowth under the trees. Broomhilda huddled with the other non-humans in the group, after a few minutes each clan left to carry out the plan discussed with the oldest fairy.

Broomhilda returned to where Logan, Luna, Stella, and their friends were sitting at the edge of the stream, their feet dangling in the sweet clear water that danced along over the stones. "They've all agreed to find their books, cast their spells, to talk to their ancestors, and to stay close to home."

"Luna and I don't have ancestors to learn from, but we have the books, gifted to us by those who walked here before us." Luna nodded as Stella continued. "We'll work it out, with our covens. Our intuition and our intentions with knowledge of our friends, that's a powerful spell in itself."

"We'll work it out together." Brigid agreed, hugging Stella. Motioning to the others seated there, in the peace of the fairy glen, she continued. "The school we attended has long been abandoned. Since Cain and his gang started stealing children and brain washing others, the eldest in our villages and towns decided, in this realm, to keep children close, teach them at home. Most of the children you see around the market are alone but protected by all the shop owners. We look after them as best we can."

"Penne and Sage have created a safe space, a school for the children we've rescued. Broomhilda helped set it up, protect it and hide it from everyone. I'm forever grateful and in your debt for that." Kai spoke to the smallest in their group. "Maybe, in time we could extend that school to teach adults who want to know more about their skills and abilities, once we finally defeat my cousin."

Chapter Five

C ain

Kai's cousin, leader of the malevolent coven, couldn't find the do gooders anywhere. His magic feelers spread out over the realm, tendrils trailing through the villages, the forests and the deepest darkest woods, though he didn't expect to find them there. Curious as to whether Kai was pretending to befriend Stella and her crew or if she'd changed alliances. "It makes sense that fae magic is hiding them for now. They must return to their villages soon; I'll find them then." He'd a habit of talking out loud, to no one in particular. None of The Coven ever spoke up about it, they wouldn't dare. Heads down, the others busied themselves with eating the food in front of them. Training sessions were exhausting, the food helped. No one wanted to pick a fight with their leader. They'd no energy left for conflict.

His finger traced the marking on his right arm. The eye in the middle of the pentagram, a mark of their coven. Some of those seated absently traced their tattoos, an automatic reaction to copy the master's actions. Cain's sigil imbued with magic, the tattoos on his coven contained no magic, except that which dulled their ability to speak out against his plans. He'd branded all the members of his coven. Those loyal to him could be found throughout all the realms, even Stella's modern world.

The children he'd captured and taught over the years. Not all but most stayed loyal to him. He grinned, his evil lopsided grin at the memory of thwarting Luna and Broomhilda back then, when he first began stealing children. It was stupidly easy. As he again traced the image, he knew people throughout the lands would feel the tingling. They'd absent mindedly trace the image on their arm too. Their connection growing stronger.

"Are you eating before our training session?" A slightly built woman with unruly and unbrushed flaming red hair, motioned for Cain to join her at one of the three long tables in the dining hall. Dark wood, from ancient trees, used to create all the furniture in the castle, held the warmth of the woods where they once grew. The castle enchantment subtle, no one could identify exactly what spell was woven into the fabric, the furniture or the walls.

Silence fell in the room, no one was willing to look at the master, lest he give them some challenge or chore that was beyond their capabilities. He smiled to himself, reading the room. He kept everyone busy, ninety percent of the time. They weren't able to get into mischief if they were too scared or occupied to think for themselves.

"Thank you, Mabel. I see you've returned from scouting the area. We look forward to your update at this afternoon's session. I can see by the dishevelled look of some of our older members, that you must've taken army skills this morning." Sword work and knife skills. Mabel, one of the founding coven members, thin as she was wiry and twice as angry. Her blood lust made her the perfect army chief. Loyal, she worked them hard and made sure their army was the best in the land.

"A motley bunch we have here to be sure. I'll knock them into line by the end of this week." Mabel stabbed a piece of meat with a fork. The young lad on her right cringed, sliding as small in his seat as he could. A snort of laughter came from the other side of the table. "Before you laugh, I suggest you learn which end of your sword to hold and which end to jab into your opponent." Mabel shot the older male a withering stare.

"After lunch we'll be practising portals and blocking enchantments." Cain's voice echoed through the dining hall. "Fae magick is powerful, but not as strong as our magic. We are the *Mark of the Thirteen*. The original thirteen founding coven members knew what they were up against. We've been beaten in the past, but this time we'll win." Cain's black aura wound its path around the gathering. The tendrils of his ego and aura an invisible finger that grabbed them, keeping them firmly in his grasp. "Free will." He said firmly, knowing that none of them had any choice in the matter. The clothes, the food and the atmosphere in the castle were constructed to keep them there. "Is part of our strength. Belief in each other and our common goal." The sound of his own voice soothed him more than anyone else. Once he started it was difficult to stop.

Chapter Six

K^{ai} "It wasn't safe for me to stay with my coven. We agreed that Penne and Sage would ensure the children's safety. I kept my cousin occupied, convinced him I'd returned, and he promised not to follow them." Kai shared her story with Stella and Luna over a meal in the tavern. Brigid convinced everyone to meet at her tavern to plan a way forward. Catherine agreed her tavern was too far on the other side of town, too close to the castle where Kai grew up.

If he's tracking me, nowhere is safe. Kai kept her fears to herself. If there was a haven anywhere, it was here with these people, who were as good as her cousin was evil.

Brigid shooed out the customers, tempting them with a plate of sweetmeat and promises of free food and drink when she opened the following day. She locked the door as the others gathered around the table loaded with breads, meats and tankards of mead.

"Everyone, this is Kai. Kai, meet Luna, Catherine, Tizzie, Logan, Blair and Angus. Brigid and Maisie, you have met before." Stella motioned for Kai to sit next to her.

"There'll be a test later." Logan quipped.

"Did you really escape the castle, twice?" Blair, the youngest of Logans' coven asked admiringly. He grabbed a piece of bread dropping it like a hot potato when Logan whacked his arm.

"Logan, stop it, let the poor lad eat his fill." Brigid admonished him.

"It took some doing." Kai answered the question posed by Blair. "I took notice of every movement, every guard and item of security my cousin has in place. I paid attention to the spells and enchantments. The only way out of the castle was to beat them at their own game. The first time took them by surprise, they didn't know I wasn't brain washed like the others. This last time proved more difficult. Cain and his cronies needed to think I'd become a willing and loyal member of the team."

"Let Kai rest and eat." Brigid spoke firmly as she passed the plate of food towards Kai. Logan and the others made a swipe at the food as it passed by them.

"Do you miss your coven?" Tizzie asked, as she nibbled on a piece of bread.

"Every single minute." Kai picked up her tankard, holding it with both hands. "It'll take him longer to find them if I'm not with them. Penne and Sage will ensure the children are safe, loved, looked after, and educated. The enchantment is strong, the fae magic will keep them safe. When they reach a certain age, they decide if they want to stay and help or go their own way."

"How many children?" Maisie asked quietly.

"At the moment about fifty." Kai counted in her head. Her heart pounded, her emotions heavy whenever she thought of her friends, and all they sacrificed to save the children. "There've been hundreds over the years, before we were old enough to help them. Cain depended on stealing them, to grow his army."

"Thank goodness I know where my children are and they're safe." As soon as the words were out of her mouth Stella regretted them. With tears in her eyes, she clasped her hands together. "I'm sorry Luna."

"Don't be. I've searched, we've searched, everywhere, across the realms for them. I've often wondered if it was the *Mark of the Thirteen* who took them, or their dad and his family. Both had reasons to make me suffer." Luna sighed; her hands twisted the piece of plaited purple cloth loosely tied around the waist of her long black dress. Under her dress, thick black leggings served to keep her warm and make moving a lot easier than in the clothing her friends wore. She was glad she'd worn them last time she'd come through the portal in the cupboard in her little house.

"Oh Luna, I'm sorry. I didn't know." Kai wanted to hug the crone but wasn't sure how well that'd be received. "Their whereabouts could be cloaked, hidden from you. It's something my cousin would do, out of spite."

"I'll never give up believing one day we'll be reunited." Luna's voice wobbled. Catherine and Tizzie wrapped their arms around her protectively.

Her magic tingling as she thought of the pain and angst inflicted on so many by her cousin, Kai said. "I can't promise to find them, but I'll do everything I can to help."

"Is it true that Cain's magic is nearly equal to Broomhilda's?" Stella asked.

"As I understand it." Catherine said as she handed out more tankards of mead, while Brigid added more bread and cheese to the platters. "Cain's family is old magic. So is Broomhilda's. The main difference being that Broomhilda's family is Fae and fairy magic is stronger than any other."

"Wouldn't he then want to steal fairy and elfin magic as well? That way he'd have it all?" Logan asked.

"You'd think so, but if he tried that, he'd lose his own power, all of it." Kai put her tankard back on the wooden bench. "Apparently it's an ancient magic law, that even he daren't cross."

A sombre silence settled over the group.

"The *Mark of the Thirteen* weren't always evil." Kai said quietly. "Selfish, greedy, and out to grow their own power and wealth, but not murderous. It's gotten worse since Cain took over as leader. I can't prove it, but I'm certain he killed my parents and his too."

"He hates women with power." Hecate spoke through Stella. "Broomhilda's power is tired. As is mine, after fighting for so long. We can channel our strength through you, the younger generation of witches. Listen, pay attention and you'll know when it's time to act."

Everyone waited for more, but Hecate kept silent.

"IT'S GOOD TO SEE THE fire in the market square didn't cause as much damage as we first thought." Brigid stood up and collected the empty platters.

Kai listened to Maisie's account of the fire in the market square, a sense of foreboding filled the pit of her stomach. It wasn't the story that gave her gooseflesh along her arms and down her legs. A cold breeze lazed in from under the bolted wooden door. Her cousin's aura, sickly, thick, choking her permeated the air entering the tavern from the town. Although she couldn't see him with her eyes, he was there, she was certain of it. In search of her, or someone else? Should she tell her new friends? Were they safe if she stayed?

"I DON'T WANT TO RISK causing harm to Stella and her friends." She told Penne and Sage. Kai noted her surroundings, the cottage hidden deep in the woods, an enchantment a veil that wouldn't keep Cain out for ever. "I can't sense him or his cronies here, yet." She was cautiously optimistic. "I guess that means we've some time to work out our long-term plan." Was there anywhere Kai and her friends could live, without the threat of Cain finding them and punishing them? He'd made a lifetime of stealing children, those he feared would grow up powerful. He brainwashed them, with promises of prosperity. Greed was a strong motivator. Those who escaped, didn't last long without being caught. If they managed to stay hidden, they were barely able to eke out a simple beggar's existence. Those forced to return, were imprisoned, never to see daylight again. The wisest chose to stay and join the army, as Cain's henchman, willing to do his bidding, no matter the cost.

"Can you tell us where you are?" Penne asked. Her blonde hair braided into a bun that wrapped around her head. Her sister Sage preferred to let her hair hang around her face. Kai's fingers touched her own shock of purple hair that stuck out from under her hood. She wasn't sure she liked short hair, but it was so much easier to look after.

"I'd better not. I'm risking enough by visiting through the fire. The less we talk about our locations, the safer we'll be. This is a quick visit, to share what I've learnt. Broomhilda spoke of a way we can undo the evil, to set free the children taken over the years. I know that numbers in the hundreds, if not more, but still, apparently it can be done, given a specific set of circumstances are met." Penne and Sage listened with wide eyes, their hearts beating as loudly as Kai's. Their connection crossed time and space; having grown up together in the castle, Sage and Penne servant daughters, best friends with the heir to the throne. Heir until Cain had wiped out a generation and claimed the throne himself. "We haven't been able to unlock any power in those we have rescued, though it's logical to assume they may possess magic. If we can unlock their power, we may be able to thwart the evil once and for all." Kai's energy buzzed, as it did when she was close to her friends. She didn't refer to them as a coven, often, she saw herself as far more practical rather than powerful.

Kai held her finger to her lips, listening to the sounds of the forest. Something was wrong. She sensed her cousin searching for her, angry, careless with his energy. Her arm rose, in a sweeping motion she blocked him, sending him on a false chase in the opposite direction. "I'm betting his ego won't let him second guess that he's on the right track."

Silence fell for a few minutes, no one wanted to break it. Penne and Sage knew Kai would need to leave soon. Kai took in her surroundings. She knew this cottage, a place she'd hidden with her friends during her first escape. The cottage had two rooms, built from wood. A few thick blankets on the floor in front of the fireplaces kept it warm, snug. The enchantment surrounding the cottage protected the building and all who sought safety.

The rooms were empty, apart from Kai and her friends. "I expected to see the children." She racked her brains, trying to remember where the secret tunnel was. Sage led her to the back corner of the second room and opened the wardrobe door. Kai held Penne and Sage's hand as they took her through the darkened tunnel.

"I'd be scared, if I didn't trust you both." Kai couldn't keep the fear from her voice, an irrational fear of the dark plagued her, since Cain imprisoned her in a wooden box when she was five.

"Oh sorry, of course." Penne picked a torch from the wall and lit it.

Kai did her best to hide her claustrophobia, but some days, it got the better of her. Memories as a child of being locked in a chest, in a cupboard, all by her cousin. She shook them away. Kai could see the walls now, and the floor. The tunnel appeared to be built into the side of a mountain. She watched, fascinated as the oil lamps on the walls sprang into life, the further they ventured into the tunnel.

"Broomhilda helped us make sure the children are safe. Her fairies and some elves created this for us, the lights, and the enchantment at the front of the cottage. No one else can see the cottage or stumble across it. From the other side this is a sheer mountain which drops away at the top into the ocean, the North Sea. A desolate part, where many sailors have lost their lives on the rocks and people have fallen off the cliffs trying to see through the fog." Sage filled in the gaps as they walked towards what appeared to be a muffled light.

Penne opened the door. Kai found herself in a huge room, a little like the dining room in her cousin's castle, their family castle, but with one huge difference. This one was filled with light and positive energy, rather than the evil that dripped from every pore of everything her cousin created.

A few small children ran and embraced her friends. One broke away and wrapped her tiny arms around Kai's legs. "Thank you." The small child whispered. "For saving me and my sisters and my brother."

The room was lined with long tables laden with fruits and breads. Children sat at the table, eating, others were reading or writing, while some ran around chasing toys that moved and rolled around the stone floor.

"The elves are teaching lessons," Sage pointed to the table where an older group of children were reading and writing. Dressed in long cream-coloured robes that looked warm and comfortable.

'A couple of fairies stayed to run the creche. They tend to our garden and will be teaching the children how to grow, cook, and live sustainably."

"Wow." This place seemed so far away from the clutches of the malevolent coven. Could their plan work? Kai didn't want to say anything that may jinx it, hoping with her heart full of gratitude for all that was good, that this would be successful.

"This is what we always hoped to achieve. It's sad that the others that were rescued weren't able to be a part of this." Sage paused, running her fingers through her blonde waves. "I'm hopeful we may be able to create a lasting solution to the problem; if we could empower these children, and somehow connect with the others, from long ago."

Kai yearned to stay here, with her friends, to pretend it was safe, and raise the children. To create a sense of adventure, a love of learning and magic, where they knew they were safe from danger. She knew that wasn't possible, yet.

"Do you have to go now?" Sage asked reading her friend's mind.

"The flames are nearly out." Kai hugged them. "It's not forever. We'll beat him. For good. It might be a while before I can visit, but we'll stay in contact through the fire."

Chapter Seven

S tella

Stella knew where her children were. "I can't always contact them, but I know they're safe, working, travelling, and enjoying their youth. The youngest two, Andie and Emily, I talk to at least once a week. The older two, Pedro and Kay, refuse to speak to me. In their opinion I'm the evil one who broke the family up years ago." Except that she wasn't, but no amount of objecting to the label could change their viewpoint.

"I have to be patient." She reminded herself, as she told her friends about her children. "They're out of harm's way. At least Broomhilda assured me there'll be no danger to them. The threat's here, in this realm."

"Days ago, the threat was in both our realms." Brigid reminded her gently.

"True. He was making a power play, here and in that realm, for power and wealth. That wasn't personal, although I fear anything he does now will be. Not only did we thwart his plans, but we freed Kai from her connection and obligation to him." An ache started in the pit of Stella's stomach. The same ache as when the children's dad took them and moved away. Brigid's words hung heavy in the air. What if Cain went after her children? Would he? Could he? It didn't bear thinking about. That image stuck firmly in her mind's eye, of her children captured, tied up in some dungeon somewhere. She clenched her fists, channelling her energy into protecting them.

"We must tread carefully." Maisie placed a tray piled with sweet pastries onto the table between them. Stella pulled herself away from the haunting image, and focused on the present, on her friend's words.

Early in the morning on the second day since Stella's return, too late to pretend everything was normal, they faced the reality of malevolence which couldn't be ignored. Still there were things they could do, to prove that the evil was not going to win.

"With some market stalls undergoing repairs, it's important I open my store today. People need a sense of normality, and clothing. It's a good thing I have some other bits and pieces available too. Not as much range as at the markets, but still." Maisie's shop had robes, dresses, shoes, leather work and some fabrics. The travellers who normally stocked the markets had left some for her to sell as well. "I'll donate a portion of the money to the stalls that are damaged, until they can re-open."

"I've put together a box of food stuffs, anyone can add to it, all the donations are going to the stallholders. Our customers have been so generous." Brigid pointed to the wicker basket that held foodstuffs and a box full of coins. "I'm taking some food to the markets later, to make sure the stallholders have at least one meal today."

"I'll take Kai to the apothecary, she can help me finish the stocktake. Don't worry, I'll be safe. They won't try the same trick twice." Stella turned to Kai. "Your cousin sent some travellers to kidnap me. They told me they were searching for herbal remedies, so I took them to my apothecary to get what they needed. That's when they took me to where I met you. Brigid and Maisie tried to warn me, but I didn't listen."

"I swear Kai was there." Stella said, pointing to the bench behind them, realising she'd provided an explanation to thin air.

"So did I." Brigid lifted the blanket, checking that Kai wasn't snuggled under it. "Where is Kai? I haven't seen her since last evening. Did she go with Luna?"

"I doubt it, Luna doesn't trust her." Maisie said.

The door to the pantry opened. "Here I am. I'd planned to surprise you with a feast for breakfast, but I fell asleep in there. It was warmer than the forest."

"The forest?"

"I can sense my cousin; I tried drawing him out to confront him. Then I decided a safer option was to make him believe I'd run away. I sent my trail far away from here, and in the opposite direction from my friends and the children. I fear he'll work it out and return soon."

Stella hugged Kai. "We'll do our best to make sure we keep everyone safe." Her stomach settled a little, though she couldn't face food. Whenever she worried about her kids, her stomach tied itself in knots. This time, even with her magic and Hecate, trepidation at facing Cain, threatened to overwhelm her.

Believe in yourself. Her intuition whispered loudly, overriding her fear.

"We meet back here, before it's dark." Maisie called as Stella and Kai headed out the door. Noticing the questioning look from Stella and Brigid, Maisie continued with a smile. "Well, I know you'll tell me not to worry and to look after my customers."

"THIS IS LIKE ONE OF the gypsy wagons, but bigger." Kai's fingers ran along the row of bottles containing mugwort, patchouli, myrrh, and frankincense.

"Most of those bottles came from one of those wagons. The traders are happy to sell me their wares, if I recommend their wagons while they are in town. It works well as we mainly stock different products anyway." Stella pointed to the row below, where the products were labelled by the ailment – headache, boils, fever, leprosy.

"Can you teach me how to use some of these? I'd be more help to Penne and Sage if I knew how to heal using these. We have a basic knowledge of first aid, but not like this." Kai never considered herself a healer, until now. Her energy tingled as she touched each bottle.

"Sure."

Out of the corner of her third eye, Stella sensed a hooded figure at the door. She turned, instinctively throwing up a strong enchantment, slamming the door shut and knocking the person a few feet away.

"Cain!" In one leap, Kai sprung out the door after her cousin. She returned a few seconds later, breathless from sprinting. "I swear there was someone there, I sensed him, Cain, but there wasn't anyone in the alley."

"Me too." Stella admitted. "I must be jumping at shadows, or ghosts."

"Not a ghost. A hologram of sorts." Both women spun around at the sound of a familiar voice.

"Flix!" Stella shouted, seeing the sprite who'd come to her aid, when she'd been kidnapped. The little creature, no bigger than Broomhilda, was dressed in crimson pants, and a long shirt, black boots, and a brown cap.

"No hugging." Flix reminded his human friend, remembering the times she'd threatened to embrace him during their last adventure. Stella hadn't yet worked out how to hug her little friend without squashing him.

"It's so good to see you. How long have you been sitting there?" Stella high fived her friend with her little finger.

"Broomhilda wanted me to protect you, again." He rolled his eyes in mock exasperation. "It looks like I was too late. If he located you by hologram he'll know where you are. Unless we can confuse the energy so its fuzzy and he can't find you again."

"How do we do that?" Kai asked, clenching her fists, anxious at the thought that Cain could find her friends.

"I hoped you knew." Flix responded, looking from Stella to Kai. "I guess I could ask Broomhilda."

"Hmm. I think Hecate knows how to blur the energy lines. Can you watch me while I follow the trail of the hologram and draw false lines back so he can't find us again?"

"Of course." Kai and Flix responded in unison.

Stella lay on the bench along the back wall and closed her eyes, opening her mind to the channel of energy. She followed the dark flow of particles, like a dust storm, gritty and dirty, along the waves until she reached the edge of the forest the farthest point from the town. The icky line transversed the valley, crossing a river and twisting around a mountain to a monstrous dark castle fort on the dark side of the mountain.

Like playing a game of cat and mouse, she jiggled her energy, and once she felt the darkness change direction to follow her light, she changed direction. Darting in and out of the trees and the forest floor, sailing up into the clouds and twisting back onto the previous trail, she saw the darkness lose the connection with her light. She returned to her friends.

"Hecate showed me where to stop, any closer to the castle and they would have captured me or traced me back here. In the air there was this line of pure energy. On our side shone pure light. On the other side, a greyness seeped across everything. It's clear Cain has a dark enchantment woven over his castle, your castle, and everyone within it. Though you didn't succumb." Stella ran her third eye over her friend. She found no evidence of the darkness she'd just witnessed, leaving her in no doubt that Kai didn't belong to the coven. "I muddied the path, turning it back onto itself, then forward and around and through an old crumbling castle ruin. Finally, I wrapped it around itself until it broke. There's no way they can follow that. I erased any trace of their energy for miles. Then I flew back here as fast as I could, blasting shut the hole the hologram bored through the village."

STELLA RECOUNTED THE story to her friends in the tavern a few hours later.

"Her magic has grown so much." Brigid marvelled to Maisie, passing a tray of tankards to a table of boisterous young men.

"In such a short space of time." Maisie agreed. "To think I was worried about her being at her apothecary."

"Okay so stop talking about me as if I'm not here, or a specimen in a jar." Stella responded. "I'd love a drink and something to eat. Astral travelling, if that's what it was, makes me tired and hungry."

"Of course." Brigid motioned for them to sit. "Are we worried about him coming back? Should we be doing something to prepare?"

Flix jumped up onto the middle of the table. "Broomhilda suggests we go about our normal business. Doing anything unusual may attract him back. She'll warn Luna and Logan to be on alert for anything unusual."

"Are the others in any danger?" Maisie wondered aloud.

"Probably, but for now we can best protect them by not contacting them. Broomhilda is making plans, and she'll let us know when we're to move onto phase two." Flix scratched his chin. "Do we know what phase two is?"

"I'm sure she'll tell us when she's ready. I'm going to spread a simple protection spell around our businesses." Stella said. "It'll be subtle, understated. Cain will be looking for something strong and shiny. My simple intention won't trigger anything, but it'll keep each of us safe from any malevolence." This knowledge, from Hecate, knowledge from deep within and long ago, came easily to Stella.

"This increased knowledge of enchantments, is Hecate? Is she with you all the time?" Brigid asked, ducking as one of the lads from the other table threw a tankard in the air. "Oi, do that again and you and your friends are out." She flicked the cloth in her hands at the table.

"Hecate's been quiet since that day, but she's always with me. Yes, the extra knowledge I have gained, is from her. Guiding me, showing me how to perform certain spells, or how to travel through time and space. It's like nothing else I've ever experienced, and very difficult to explain." Stella mused. "Broomhilda said I'm not in any danger from Hecate. I believe her."

"Well as long as you are okay. Also, you're not leaving the tavern. None of us are. We can all stay here tonight. Right Brigid?" Stella knew Maisie would be freaking out about the possibility of something bad happening again. Brigid nodded.

Secretly pleased not to be alone, and glad her tiny friend had returned, Stella smiled. "Don't be fooled by Flix's small stature, he protected me, kept me safe from the malevolent coven on several occasions. He protected me from Kai, before we became friends."

"While I'm here I'll keep you all safe." Flix confirmed.

Chapter Eight

S tella

"I almost forgot." Stella reached into the basket of books and papers on the floor by the bench where she sat. The hour was late and the couple of oldies were left in the tavern, hugging their tankards, savouring the last drops before the landlord called closing time. Brigid was lenient, though she'd be gently sending them on their way soon.

"What have you got there?" Maisie leant over, nearly knocking over a platter of cheese.

"I hoped to find information about the coven, in amongst the notes and books at my shop." She spread the books on the table in front of them. "I didn't get a chance to look through these. I thought we could do it now it's quietened down in here." The light wasn't great, the oil lantern burning down to the end of its wick. Brigid reached around behind her and dragged a couple of larger candles to the end of the table.

For the next hour, the only sound to be heard in the tavern was the turning of pages. Brigid didn't have to evict the older customers, the lack of attention by the owner, who ignored their harrumphs encouraged them to find shelter elsewhere.

As Stella rifled through a pile of books and papers she didn't remember bringing with her, her intuition showed her a series of drawings. She flicked through each page, looking for the images, a series of arrows, and symbols that reminded her of a tattoo she'd seen somewhere.

A tiny tapping noise distracted her. Flix was sitting on the bar, his foot banging the bar, so tiny that it was little louder than a finger on a table.

Brigid, Maisie, and Kai were curled up under their respective blankets, they're breathing even as they slumbered. Stella couldn't blame them, she squinted to read the ancient texts by the fading candlelight, raising her finger to her lips for Flix to stop kicking. Gently laying Kai's head back onto her blanket, rather than her shoulder, she slipped over to Flix. "What's up?"

"Are we worried that you've skills and memories that are part of the existence of a powerful witch from centuries ago?" Flix, scratched his tiny chin.

"It doesn't feel like she's taken over. I don't even hear her voice in my head. It's more an added layer of knowledge and skill." Stella saw the sprite's eyebrows furrow; a sign he wasn't convinced. "I promise to talk to Broomhilda about it next time I see her, or earlier if something odd happens."

Flix rolled his eyes. "Your definition of odd is a little different to mine. So, what's in the books?" Plonking himself down at the side of the book in front of Stella. "It looks like gibberish to me."

Stella closed the book, reading the words on the cover, and re-opened it to the first page. "It appears to be a book of spells to brainwash people, to force them to do your bidding." Stella shuddered, and Flix sprung back away from the tome. "This next one, as white and shiny as that one is dark, contains spells to stop being brainwashed, or to remove a brainwash spell." The book in Stella's hand shimmered and shone, its own inner light source in the dim light in the tavern.

Flix eyed the books cautiously. "There must be lots of different ways to cast those spells, those books aren't exactly thin."

Stella nodded "It's curious that a book showing me what the malevolent coven uses to cast their spell, plus a book outlining a way to reverse it, both appeared in my shop. Can Hecate make things manifest, from beyond, wherever she is?" Stella wished she could slip out and tuck the books in the wooden vault which mysteriously appeared under her work bench. Before she finished the thought, the books vanished.

"A cloaking spell?" Flix asked. "I know you put the books somewhere, but from where I'm standing, they disappeared."

"I wished I could return the books to the shop, to where I found them today, in the large wooden box under my workbench."

Flix shook his head, reading her mind. "You're not going back there to find out."

Before Stella could say, "You're right. I'm not." The space in front of her spun and twisted. She felt Flix jump into her arms as she instinctively wrapped them around herself. Stella had travelled through portals, through time on several occasions. This was nothing like that. Everything in front of her blurred, and after a few seconds in darkness, everything that was blurry became clear again. Her apothecary materialised in front of her.

"What the heck was that?" The sprite took a step back from where he landed, on the floor under the work bench. "I thought you'd tell me if I was going to end up in a portal, a time slip, or a black hole."

"I'd no idea that was going to happen." Stella held out her hand. Flix climbed up on it, balancing himself as she placed him on the top of the wooden work bench. She squatted and picked up the book she'd landed on. Flix moved as far away as he could, a look of horror on his face.

"Poisonous herbs, hallucinogens, herbs for nightmares, illness, oh and the antidote for each." She quickly popped the book into the wooden box at her feet. "You know you can't get sick from the book." Stella told Flix.

"Not taking any chances."

"Two more to go." Hoping to reassure her friend, she picked up two other books as they appeared at her feet. "These aren't so bad. How to cloak whole communities and how to find them, how to take magic and how to restore it. I think Hecate is guiding me, revealing the secrets of the coven plus how to fix their evil enchantments. I'll show Kai and see if she recognises the books."

"Are you sure we trust her?" Flix asked. "Why would Hecate bring us here to read these, rather than at the tavern with the others?"

"I don't know why, but yes. I do trust Kai. She's not a part of that coven. She's spent her whole life trying to undo their work."

Stella stopped, putting her finger to her lips, as the thunder of footsteps running past made them both jump. Loud voices, yelling words Stella couldn't quite understand, curious, she picked Flix up, before he could protest and tucked him in the pocket of her coat. She joined the gathering crowd watching the scene in front of them.

"Little beggar tried to steal from Big Al's stall. Must be new round here, no one would be silly enough to steal from him." A weedy little man, his long hair tied in a rat's tail spoke near Stella. "Even in the dark, it's crazy to try, especially with the stall holders working through the night to get their stalls ready for business.

"I've heard of Big Al. Doesn't he trade in artifacts from the orient, magic lamps and wands and the like?" A plump woman wearing a leather apron asked.

"Yeah, not exactly items that a thief could hide in his pocket." The weedy man scratched his head. "Haven't seen the young one here before. A mystery where he's come from. We're used to runaways, but this feels different. The town's on edge after all the goings on, and the fire."

"You don't think he's been sent here, by someone who wants to do more harm? Here to cause some sort of mischief." A skinny woman spoke, her arms full with a sleeping bairn. She wobbled a little, as if she'd been holding him for a while.

Stella shook her head slowly, before speaking loudly enough for those around her to hear. "I don't think we can afford to think the worst of everyone. We do need to be cautious and watch out for the evil that is lurking around, but not turn on each other." A murmur spread through the crowd at her words. "But we can't accuse people, children, of evil doing if we aren't sure whether they're malicious or unfortunate. Fear, panic, and drama creates more of the same, and lets those evil doers get a hold."

"So then, what's the solution?" Yelled a voice at the back of the crowd.

"Follow our intuition. Look out for each other. Stay calm."

"I don't suppose you have a calming potion in your shop? Or a spell you could cast over the town and calm everyone down?" Asked the mother holding the child.

"Or one to reveal who is honest and who isn't?" The weedy man added.

"While those spells may work, it'd be too easy to manipulate. I have potions and oils to aid with anxiety if anyone would like a sample, free of charge." Flix kicked her from inside the pocket of her coat. Stella wasn't about to charge for a potion if it meant she could help keep a level of peace in the town, no matter how many times the tiny sprite kicked her.

Logan walked up, dragging a youth of about eighteen by his arm, firmly but not unkindly. "Don't s'ppose you want an apprentice?" he asked gloomily. "I convinced Big Al this blighter wouldn't get off without consequences, but I don't particularly want him hanging around me."

Stella knew that Logan was due to travel to the other realm to talk to his contacts about Cain's plans. Intuition told her he'd normally take on the youngster, if he was sticking around.

"Brigid or Catherine might need a hand to clean, if you're passing by their taverns." She suggested.

THE HOODED FIGURE WATCHED with interest. The youth wasn't one of his though maybe he could be. No wonder these humans were no threat to him, not really. It appeared they were merely trying to look after themselves, rather than demonstrating any coordinated or united purpose.

He mustn't underestimate Stella though. There was something odd about her. He couldn't work out what was bugging him about the way she held herself, how she spoke to the crowd. He didn't like not knowing something. He was tempted to throw a handful of his secret black salt ash over the crowd to reveal her secret, but he didn't want to draw attention to himself.

Swearing under his breath a curse so old even he couldn't remember what it originally meant, he swung his cloak tightly around himself and vanished. No one paid any attention except for a tiny fairy, who'd been going about her business, collecting teeth from under the pillows of sleeping bairns. She dropped her velvet pouch of coins when the breeze of his cloak flung her around in a circle.

Chapter Nine

L una

On the days when she missed her children more than she could bear, the old crone loved digging in her garden, the feel of the dirt on her hands settling her nerves and cooling her emotions. Life in medieval Scotland meant giving up the garden she'd so lovingly created in her cottage back in Australia. Tizzie knew how much Luna was suffering without her healing space and managed to find a few old barrels, some dirt from a nearby farm, and seeds from local traders.

With hot tears stinging her eyes, Luna dragged one of the barrels around to where she wanted it, at the back of her shop, which opened onto her workshop. The gift meant so much to her, she didn't want to leave them out where they might get stolen. "Thank you."

Catherine and Tizzie followed, with the other barrels. "You're welcome." They said together.

"We know it helps, spending time in your garden. This isn't the same as the beautiful healing space you created in your other garden, but hopefully it will help." Catherine wrapped her arms around her friend.

"We've found a trader who can source rarer seeds and plants. I'll introduce you next time they come through town, and you can tell them what you need. My treat." Tizzie gently wiped a tear from her friend's cheek.

All three women knew Luna could conjure up any seed, plant or healing potion if she wanted to. If needed, she could whip up lotions for any ailment or problem. "Thank you isn't enough." Luna swiped away the rivulet of salty tears as they reached her lips. She knew she didn't have to mention how at certain times during any month the loss and grief was overwhelming, even all these years later. As if her children had been torn away from her yesterday and not more than twenty years ago. Twenty-eight years, three months and thirteen days to be exact. No trace in any land. Christmas, birthday's, celebrations, the days when the loss stung the worst.

"Are we ready for tonight?" Luna asked. "I know I've been distracted, but see, the plants are already making me feel better, focus, and see more clearly." She ran her fingers lovingly through one of the pots of dirt. Her mind imagining the plethora of herbs she could grow.

"Preparations for the full moon ritual are well under way. We've everything organised. Logan might be late, but the others will be here. Maisie and Brigid want it extra special for Stella, after she missed the celebrations at the last dark moon." Catherine remembered the worry and pain when Stella had been taken, sent back to her world, missing the first dark moon she was due to celebrate with her coven.

"Are we to expect Kai to be part of the festivities?" Luna asked as she stacked the bags of seeds beside the barrels her hands itching to get into the soil.

"Stella trusts her." Catherine pointed out. "It'll do no harm to include her."

"One of the *Mark of the Thirteen* celebrating with us? We could give her the benefit of the doubt I suppose. It's called keeping our enemies close, I think." Luna mused. "Maybe we can learn valuable information from her to thwart her coven."

"I'm sure if we ask her, she'll share any information she has that will help us defeat her cousin." Tizzie suggested.

"If she won't volunteer the information maybe Broomhilda can put a spell on her to be truthful." Luna muttered. She saw her friends both roll their eyes. She didn't care, she didn't easily trust newcomers.

Luna's unspoken question, that she daren't ask out loud, or even to herself, was, would Kai know what could have happened to her children so long ago. If Kai was to be trusted, maybe there was a glimmer of hope after all.

THE HOODED FIGURE KNEW the answer to the question that the old crone wasn't game to ask aloud. He sneered as he watched her, hands in the dirt, weaving her magic. He saw her two friends, followed them as they walked back to their tavern and the dress shop respectively. They were no match for him and his coven. Mere amateurs, no matter how long they'd been practising their magic. What had they achieved over the years? Sure, they banished him once. It'd taken twenty-seven years to escape that exile. On the last two occasions, despite the addition of Stella, he spat as he thought of the newcomer, they'd fail to keep him bound. His magic was stronger, none of them were a match for him. He'd his castle and his followers, all in one place, all working continually and constantly, together - for one reason – to do his bidding.

BROOMHILDA WAS WATCHING the watcher, cloaked so he'd no idea she was observing and listening to most of his thoughts as they echoed aloud in the line she had drawn lightly between them. Her sister Gertrude, the tooth fairy, alerted her to the evil presence. The oldest fairy followed the stench to find that the malevolent one had indeed ventured far from his comfort zone. His ego blinded him to the idea that anyone would discover him.

His thoughts weren't a pleasant place for a fairy to be. She was disturbed by the depth of his greed. She persisted, and one thought in particular gave her hope. Maybe she'd found a way to defeat him after all.

Chapter Ten

Broomhilda

A plan formed in the fairy's brain as she flew over the fairy glen. Cain insisted on keeping everyone close, in one place, to control them. His strength in numbers, had zero to do with community spirit. She needed to call everyone together, but she hesitated, weighing up the pros and cons of the idea that came to her as she listened to Cain's ramblings. Having everyone located in one place could make it too easy for them to be wiped out in one attack. On the other hand, there was power in numbers, and if they were cautious, it could work to their advantage. What should she do?

The council members may argue about which option was best. Each a leader in their clans, with strong opinions on how to proceed. She needed to work through all the options before she called them together again. Did Cain think he could sense weakness? How much time did she have? Were Cain's plans already in place or did they have time to make their own? That was the question.

"I guess we could move into the castle and prepare for war. But then we leave the town defenceless." Broomhilda leant against the ancient tree, her oldest friend, listening to the whisperings, the breeze and the multitude of creatures who called the fairy glen home. "It's true, with all of us in the castle, the town won't be under threat, whereas with Luna and Stella in their apothecaries he'll come for them there. We can place an extra strong protection enchantment around the town, similar to the ancient spell that keeps the fairy glen hidden and safe." She nodded as the whisperings from the sage of long ago shared some secrets meant for the fairies' ears only. Hours later, she knew there to be one solution to the predicament they were faced with.

"I must trust the combined wisdom of the council. That's why it exists, so I don't have to shoulder all the responsibility myself." She told her sister, who'd called to check up on her after collecting the teeth hidden under the pillows of sleeping children.

"I'm glad you aren't making the decision alone. I'm off to catch a few hours' sleep, unless you need me." Gertrude flew off to her fairy home, a tiny cottage on the fairy's estate.

Broomhilda waved her off. "Sleep well sister. I'll call on you if I need to." The sisters hadn't always enjoyed a close friendship, but with age comes understanding, and they were both so old that they appreciated their sibling for many reasons.

The call to reconvene hadn't surprised anyone. They gathered, eager to help yet dreading what was to come. Fairies and elves jostled to the front to see Broomhilda. The taller in the council stood back further to give them room.

"I want to assure you dear fae and elfin folk, that Cain and his followers are not after you. He's wary of your powers. I've seen this truth in his thoughts." It'd amused her that he feared them. A little like elephants fearing mice. "I've been able to gauge what the man is thinking, what his next actions are likely to be." She focused on the humans among the council. "Unfortunately, the threat to our towns is a serious one. He's on the hunt for those of us who've bested him, getting bolder about it. It's time to get serious about our approach. No matter what way you look at it, we must prepare for war."

An uncomfortable ripple ran through the gathering. "How?" The chorus of voices asked.

"That's up to the collective views of this group. I propose that my family castle to be the base for our plans. Stella, Luna and your sisters, could relocate there. One of Cain's delusions, that he's far superior, with his community in one place, to train and plan and come at us from a position of strength – could be one of his weaknesses. While it may be easier for him to attack us if we are located together, it'd be more productive for us to train as a team. If we do this, it takes some of the pressure off our towns. The Coven will be more likely to attack wherever Luna and Stella are, if they are in the castle, the villagers are less likely to become targets. There's an enchantment we can place around the villages, to protect them from those with malicious intent." Broomhilda paused, waiting to see what the members of the council thought.

Stella looked around at the others. "To me, it makes sense that we consolidate, especially if we need to prepare for war. It'd be easier to train if we're together. I understand the dangers of having us all in one place, but the benefits overweigh the negatives at this stage. We won't become complacent, and we aren't trying to control a whole heap of people." She turned to Kai. "Would you join us, and help us? You've seen how they train."

Kai nodded. "I'm humbled you ask, and yes of course. I'd do anything to stop them." She said quietly.

"Could we set the castle up with markets stalls, so we have the food, drink and supplies we need? But keep the shops and markets open in town too? For those who stay behind." Tizzie asked.

"That might be a good way to encourage others to join us, if they want to, there's food and drink and other items available." Maisie agreed. "For those who want to help, we shouldn't try to coerce anyone into fighting against Cain."

"Free will, always free will." Luna stated, glaring at Kai as she did so.

"Do we just go about our days as normal or is there something we can do to prepare for the worst?" Punk asked. Many of the fae and elfin murmured their agreement with his question.

"We don't want to be caught unawares." A small elf in light green clothes said softly.

"Remember what we spoke about before?" Stella spoke gently, crouching to be close to the magical being. "Stay home, look after your families. Enact protection spells. Stay alert, but as calm as possible." Stella's words calmed the gathering of small folk. Some still had furrowed brows, and crossed arms, but many were nodding their heads.

"She's right." Broomhilda mustered the last ounce of her strength. Every limb ached. "I called this meeting to confirm how we could proceed with the least impact. It's the humans who must make the preparations. The rest of us, to remain aware. I'll keep everyone informed in the usual way." The fairy raised her arms and thousands of tiny stars sprinkled down on those who'd travelled to the glen. Each elf, fairy, and other enchanted creature reached out and grabbed a star, disappearing instantly.

"Their stars take them home." Brigid told Stella as they stared at the blank spot where seconds before had stood so many magical beings.

"Is there a magic that can replicate our shops at the castle, so we don't have to move everything?" Maisie asked.

Although she knew Maisie wasn't serious, it made Broomhilda smile to be able to tell her; "It's been done. If you'd like, I've fairy folk standing by to serve in your establishments in the village, in your absence, temporarily." She added hastily seeing the look on Luna's face.

Luna frowned. "That's all well and good but seriously how do we grow our army? If we're serious about preparing for war, we need more than half a dozen in the ranks. I refuse to brainwash people." The crone twirled around, lost her balance and fell on her bottom on a rock cushioned with moss.

Stella placed her hand on her friend's arm, with a little of Hecate's power she was able to calm her. "I want to thank you Broomhilda for organising this. I think I speak for the six of us," She looked at her friends, "We'd like to take you up on your offer of some temporary assistance in our businesses." She turned to face Luna. "I don't like the idea of fighting, or building an army, but nothing else we've tried has worked. They keep coming at us, threatening us and those we love." She motioned to those remaining in the glen to sit with her beside the stream. She waited until everyone settled before continuing. "Last night Hecate showed me some books. How to brainwash people and how to clear the brainwashing, how to poison and how to heal. I'd never seen the books before."

"I wasn't a fan." Flix poked his head up from his hiding spot in the pocket of her coat. "But even I could see Hecate was showing us how we could win this war. We must win." He finished emphatically.

"If you'll let me join you, I can show you exactly how Cain and Mabel train their armies. Everything I know, I'll share with you." Kai spoke quietly, aware that she still had to earn their trust.

"Your knowledge is invaluable. Thank you for agreeing to share with us." Stella hugged her friend. "When we've moved into the castle, we'll need to train. I can teach how to use spells and potions. Brigid, can you use your skills to train in warfare, using weapons? Maisie, can you teach those who want to know how to hide in plain sight? Kai can you help each of us make sure we are aware of how they do things?"

Kai and the others nodded.

"What about Catherine, Tizzie, and I, and Logan when he returns?" Luna asked. Her fingers were twirling around a stray piece of cloth that was hanging from the sleeve of her robes.

"We're planning to teach more than warfare, aren't we?" Catherine said. "I mean, we need to teach basic magic to those who want to help. Not all the villagers learnt like we did."

"I can weave magic into materials and clothes and teach them how to change our appearance." Tizzie, gently held Luna's fingers, calming her friend down. "Luna, you'd be perfect at teaching how to recognise plants that can poison us, plants that can heal us and how to make antidotes." Luna grinned, loving the idea of getting her hands dirty again.

The oldest fairy watched her friends, for that was what these humans were to her. As the sunlight dimmed, she knew the darkness wasn't far away. A couple of robins remained near the stream, their lyrical chatting a little eerie in the stillness of the early evening. A mouse scurried along over the rocks, anxious to make it home before the dark crept in. "It's time to make the move. It gets cold here once the sun makes way for the moon. Logan will return tomorrow. I've sent a message for him to come to the castle." Broomhilda hopped onto a branch above their heads. Exhaustion started to seep into her bones, a sign she needed to rest and not get caught out here.

"You need to rest." Hecate's knowledge prompting Stella to speak softly to the oldest fairy. "You can ride in my pocket with Flix." She suggested.

CAIN STORMED THROUGH the market square, the residue of his anger shoving people aside and knocking stalls over. He was invisible, so no one could see what was happening. They put it down to one of those things that happened, like the fire, when those with magic played nearby. Why weren't they scared and trembling in their boots he wondered briefly before remembering why he was cranky in the first place. Where were they? He could find no trace of Stella, Luna or Kai.

As Broomhilda hopped in beside Flix she felt his anger and frustration on the breeze that gently fluttered around the glen. He'd never penetrate this far in, his evil too dark for the fae magic. At least she hoped so.

Chapter Eleven

K^{ai} She must be dreaming. Kai could think of no other reason why she was standing in the middle of the dining hall in the castle with her cousin and his cronies. This couldn't be real, as she seemed to be invisible to those standing around, and seated, sharing food and mead. Loud, much yelling, celebrating, slapping each other on the back. "Well done!" "Victory is ours." "A good fight." Snippets of conversations between Cain, her second in charge, Mabel with the flaming red hair, and others dressed in Cain's signature armour floated past. She daren't get closer.

A flicker of light caught her eye. Kai watched as lights clicked on, over the heads of some of the coven. Like a beacon signalling a lighthouse, just inside their auras, a blue green hue, shimmering like a warning or a clue to a missing piece of a puzzle. Intuitively Kai knew the lights were guiding her to those who'd been taken as children.

As soon as she made that connection in thought form, she found herself in the marketplace in a bustling market town. Many travellers, clients, and market owners were jostling for a place at the best stocked stalls. Kai noticed the blue green hue above the heads of some travellers. Others had an orange light shimmering above their heads. A third colour came into focus, as Kai observed the market. A deep purple, immediately Kai thought of royalty and Stella.

If the green blue hue were the lost children, what did the other colours mean? If someone was a lost child and gifted, did they have multiple colours? Did the colours vary depending on whether they had powers or not, which powers they held and whether they used their powers for good or evil?

The visons left Kai with more questions than answers. She closed her eyes, hoping to find herself back in her bed. In that dream state, half asleep, comfy, yet knowing there was work to be done, Kai tossed and turned, wishing she could get comfortable, stop that nagging feeling, a stabbing pain in her lower back. She sat up with a jolt.

Broomhilda was right. He was here. So close. She hated him with every part of her body, for what he'd done to her, her family and friends, and all the innocents he'd corrupted. Kai considered taking a chance, returning to the coven, to pretend to be on his side against the world. Problem was if he didn't believe her, she wasn't sure she'd be strong enough to escape a third time. Staying safe, and helping her friends was the wisest move for now. Kai counted back from one hundred, a trick she used many times to get to sleep in the castle of her childhood.

"CAN I WEAVE A SPELL that can track him? So that we know what he's up to." Kai asked. She and Stella were helping Broomhilda cast the spell to cloak the town. Although Cain visited the town on multiple occasions, the fae magic blurred the lines enough that he wouldn't be able to follow his own tracks. A veil on the roads entering and leaving the market town would confuse anyone with less than pure intent, causing them to lose their way in a dense fog.

"I'm not taking any chances, after last time, when the travellers kidnapped you." The ancient fairy stated. "To answer your question Kai, yes, we could track him, but it may give him a way to follow and track us."

Kai shuddered. "I don't want that. I feel the pull of that coven, some days more than others. They're getting angry. Oh, but I must tell you, I think I found a clue, something important." She stopped, staring at the space above Stella's head. "I thought so."

Hecate's voice, in Stella's head, yet it was Stella's voice that responded to her friend. "If you're seeing the colours in their auras, you're truly one of us and not part of their evil. I, Hecate, cast an enchantment years ago. If there came a time when Cain grew too powerful to defeat through banishment and exile, people's true motives would be revealed. Clues, tangible signs we would see or know to help us win. You have only pure intent, or you wouldn't be the one to see it. You could even fool him, as long as your intentions stay pure.

"The blue green colour above some of those in his coven are the lost children." Kai told them. "The orange hue means something, and deep purple means old magic, like you have."

"I see the purple above you, now you mention it, shimmering at the top of your aura." Stella said with wonder. Kai couldn't help it, she raised a hand and felt above her head, as if expecting to feel the colour. Sheepishly she retuned her hand to her side.

AN HOUR LATER, KAI sat quietly in one of the quiet garden spaces that surrounded the castle, ready to visit her friends. When she slowly opened her eyes after chanting the words that would take her to the cabin in the woods, instead of the school she expected to see, she found herself back in the castle of her childhood. Luckily no one seemed to be able to see her.

"I've had enough of their nonsense!" Cain exploded.

His henchman, fair skinned, tall and blonde, his clammy pallor made him look like a sickly child. He shook as he held out a tankard of mead. "Here my lord, to quench your thirst and refresh you from your travels."

Cain eyed his aide, a grabbed the tankard, sculling the contents in one go. "More." He commanded. The tankard filled itself to the brim with dark brown liquid. The skinny man jumped back, his blonde hair sticking on end like he'd had a fright. Maybe he was new to the ways of the coven and its master. Kai didn't recognise him, but there were often new recruits arriving from around the realm.

"We must prepare for war!" he sculled the tankard. "More!" he shouted drinking the entire contents of the third mug full of the bittersweet brown fluid.

"I'll call back all the regiments. We can grow the castle space if we need to." The man was merely parroting back what his master had said to him a few days ago, but it served to stroke Cain's ego.

She felt his anger calm, as he considered his options. "Yes. Good. Call back everyone. Incentives for getting back the quickest."

KAI FELT IT. THE PULL to return home, sent out to all who'd lived between the castle walls. As if a vine had wrapped itself around her foot, trying to pull her under a muddy, sodden riverbed. She'd never considered the castle home; it's always been a prison to her.

"This could come in handy." She told Stella what had happened as they sat down to eat, in the area Brigid and Catherine had set up as a tavern. "If I can spy on them, without them knowing it, we can figure out what they are up to."

"True, but it'd be better if you could control it. After all, you said you wanted to visit Penne and Sage, and you ended up at the castle." Stella considered Kai's words. "Your magic is strong. It took you there, so you'd know about the pull to return to the castle, so it wouldn't catch you off guard."

"DO I BOTHER TRYING to call your cousin home? After all, she made it clear she wasn't willing to stay last time." The blonde man, whose name was Stix, asked the master. He jumped as the master bellowed his response.

"Call her back anyway, tell her we'd welcome her back, as long as she proved her loyalty and see what happens."

Kai heard this interaction, as if she'd a television or radio on in the background. Grateful that her ancestors were warning her what was happening in the castle. As the words faded, she tried again to contact her true coven, her friends of so many years. This time the connection worked.

I've come back to let you know I must go away for a while." She hugged her friends so tightly she felt them squirm. Loosening her grip she asked, "How are they coping?" indicating the courtyard where children were running around chasing the bubbles that were pouring from the top storey window.

"Settling in well. The fae have been great. Teaching us spells and incantations. We have a few elves, sharing wood knowledge, trees, plants, animals, that sort of thing. A couple of the children are from the woodlands homes and there is comfort in that for them." Penne answered.

"Are you sure you can't stay this time?" Sage asked, reaching for her friend's hand, and grasping it tightly.

"I'd like to, but I need to help the others rid our realm of the threat once and for all. Yes, it's come to that. I may need to go back in undercover if he'll believe it, and yes before you ask, I'll be safe."

"Stay, for one night?" Sage asked.

The fire warm, welcoming. Kai's heart rose, watching the innocence of the small children as they danced around the fire, each with a fairy wand as a sparkler shooting electricity into the air. Their clothes made of summer material woven by fairies from rose petals and daisies, each tunic different pastel shades, pale blue, lemon, jade, pink, and lilac. On their feet, white balls of fluff as they bounced around. They'd never forget their parents, but the pain of how they lost them would ease as time grew and painful memories were replaced by happy ones. Not replaced, that's the wrong word she thought, thinking of Luna and Stella and their losses.

"Can we communicate by fire?" Penne asked, gazing into the mesmerising flames as they danced in front of them.

"Maybe. Let me contact you first. He's getting stronger, but so am I. I'll be with Stella and the others. Their magic is powerful, pure and fierce, different from his malevolence. I think together we might have a chance of defeating him."

Chapter Twelve

S tella

Not again! Stella groaned as she felt herself being dragged away, out of the comfort of her bed, where she'd just snuggled down. After a long and tiring day, she'd hope to fall asleep easily. Broomhilda's castle was so large, everyone was afforded the luxury of their own rooms for now. Maisie fretted about them not being together. Stella assured her friend of the safety of all who stayed within Broomhilda's castle walls.

She closed her eyes, telepathically sending a message to Brigid and Maisie. Before she could let them know what was happening, she felt a hand on her shoulder. She opened her eyes. Flix put a finger to his lips. She spun around to work out what was happening.

Kai!

Only it wasn't Kai, not on purpose. Kai was standing to one side of a huge stone column in a castle like Broomhilda's. Were they in Cain's castle? If so, how?

She amended the message to her coven.

Not in danger after all. I'll explain tomorrow morning.

Stella and Kai were in a large dining hall. There was a lot of noise, as at least fifty people were seated at long tables, talking as they wolfed down food from platters piled up with sweet meats, cheeses and bread. Tankards clinked, Men and women aged from late teens through to middle age, all dressed in tunics that while they weren't identical, they were matched in some way. Colours, gold threads, trims. Also, as Kai had described, there were little bulbs of lights above the heads of some of the younger ones.

It was rowdy, raucous, and to Stella it felt like a party, no, an orgy of some sort. Kai focused on the group of people with the colours of blue and green above their heads. Stella of the same opinion as Kai, that these were some of the missing children. Concentrating on those closest to her, Stella couldn't work out if they were willing participants or there under duress.

Some of the older people in the room had orange and brown hues above their heads. Stella shivered. The discontent oozed off them. The darker the aura the more nastiness that emanated from them. Where had these lights come from? Kai mentioned she hadn't seen them before. Was Hecate, or someone else, helping by providing this additional level of information?

Watch, look, listen

She heeded the words, from Hecate, her knowledge appearing like a voiceover or additional narrative. She paid attention.

The coven's castle. She smelt it, their aura. Up to that second when the pungent aroma assaulted her nostrils, she hadn't known she could smell a person's aura or that a coven collectively could put out such a strong stench. The evil intent of those in the confined space, made her stomach heave. She popped her hand over her mouth.

It was easy to pick their leader, the master as he liked to be called. His clothes were embossed with golden thread. His tunic was blacker than anything else she'd ever seen. At least now she knew what he looked like. Knowing the types of clothes they wore may also come in handy.

Stella felt the anger in Hecate, bubbling away in her veins. Worried that she may give her position away if she burst into flames, she concentrated on being calm. Her and Kai would be no match in a fight against the people in the dining hall. The noise and the smell in the room worked to their advantage; after all no one would be able to penetrate the coven's castle. Their guard was down. They were celebrating their win before it occurred.

Kai turned and nodded to her, signalling it was time to go. The image in front of Stella faded, a couple of seconds the soft blankets under her legs told her she was safely back in her bed where she'd started. The blanket felt so comfy, so safe, she resisted the urge to go and find Kai. It could wait until the morning.

THE NEXT MORNING AN atmosphere, excitement tinged with sadness permeated the castle. Stella couldn't shake the sensation as she entered the tavern in the castle, to break the fast with her friends.

"Where've you been? I came searching for you early this morning, but you weren't in your room. I started to get worried." Maisie surrounded her in a huge hug.

"Sorry, I didn't mean to scare you. I went for a walk outside. I find it calming and centring whenever I can I pop outside to spend a few minutes in nature." Stella told the truth, omitting the vision she'd shared with Kai. Should she tell the others about her visions? Why had she refrained from telling Luna about her dream of the crone's children? Did she doubt the intentions of the visions? Today, she could talk to Broomhilda, and Kai and work out the significance of her insights.

"Have you visited the apothecary set up for you and Luna? It's bigger than I thought, though it needs to be big enough to teach a class." Maisie mused.

"Yes! It's got everything we'd ever need. I'm looking forward to spending more time there today." Stella looked around. The tavern had two bar benches, both stood tall, made of a dark thick wood that felt warm to touch. Ten long table benches, made from the same wood, with seats on either side filled the rest of the room. A fire blazed in a large hearth shaped out of the stone wall. The tavern would easily fit a hundred people.

Stella noticed a large wooden door behind the bar area. "Is that the door to the larder?"

As if on cue, the door opened. Brigid entered carrying a tray of fruit. Most of the pieces Stella didn't recognise. Medieval food differed greatly from modern day. She guessed the large chunks of fleshy fruits were pre-cursors to the peaches, pears and apples she was used to. Citrus of some kind was also represented, and large red grapes, much darker than those she was used to.

"A larder, and cellar, a cool room and kitchen." Maisie said, as Brigid put the platter on one of the tables.

"There is so much room out the back there, it's amazing." Brigid added.

"Where are Luna, Catherine and Tizzie? I thought they'd be here already." Stella picked up one of the smaller pieces of citrus, and tentatively licked it. The sweet taste surprised her, having expected the sourness of a lemon, or at least tart like a lime.

"Luna wanted to make sure that their side of the town was protected. She doesn't trust anyone to do a job, she needs to do it for herself. I mean that as a compliment." Brigid said laughing at the look on Stella's face. "You wouldn't have tasted some of our food before."

"No, but it's delicious. Not at all what I expected." She chewed the rest of the citrus, which almost melted in her mouth.

Before she could reach for another segment of fruit to try, a loud bang shook the walls of the room they were in. Instinctively Stella pushed her hands out in front of her; her feet slipped, and she landed on her bottom on the cobblestone floor.

Chapter Thirteen

Stella

As the dust settled back on the ground, Stella noticed she wasn't the only one on the floor. Maisie and Brigid looked just as surprised to find themselves covered in a fine layer of stone powder. Nothing else appeared out of place in the room, nothing else had fallen to the floor. She scrambled to her feet, gingerly, but didn't feel any pain. She held out a hand to each of her friends. As they stood, on wobbly feet, they brushed the dust off their clothes.

"What was that?" Maisie asked, her voice as wobbly as her legs.

"Let's sit down, in case it happens again." Brigid suggested.

"Great idea." Stella gratefully eased herself onto one of the wooden seats. Maisie and Brigid sat opposite.

Before Stella could think of any reason why the castle would shake, the door swung open with a bang. Stella felt her friends jump, as did she, fists clenched ready to fight an unknown assailant, until they discovered the culprit.

"Kai!" All three women yelled at the same moment.

"Are you ladies all right? I didn't mean to cause that bang. The door, I mean, but also the bigger explosion. I thought Cain had found us, and I threw his magic back onto himself to keep him away. Then I woke up, realised I'd been dreaming. I hope he didn't feel it, or that if he did, he can't trace it." Kai spoke breathlessly, as if she'd ran a marathon.

"Sometimes it's difficult to tell the difference between a vision and reality. Especially when we visit places in our dreams as well." Stella motioned for Kai to join them.

"Oh my gosh. Was that part real? Did I drag you with me when I spied on Cain last night?" Kai's voice was still shaky.

Brigid put her hand on Kai's. "You're safe. We all are. Cain isn't here, and if he tries to find us, well we'll send him packing." Brigid fired up, as she often did when someone she cared about was hurt or in danger.

"Rewind to that part about travelling to the coven please." Maisie spoke softly.

"Oh that. It was nothing. Somehow Kai and I ended up spying on Cain and his lot. I saw the lights above their heads. I think it's useful, not sure why, but it'll come in handy in the future I think."

"I didn't mean to take you with me, but I'm glad you got to see those lights." Kai pointed to the plate of fruit. "May I have some fruit please?"

"Help yourself." Brigid passed the plate over to Kai.

"How does that work?" Stella asked Kai. "The astral travelling? Did you mean to? And how come they didn't see us?"

Kai shrugged her shoulders. "I don't know the answers. The first time it happened it came as a surprise to me, that I ended up back at the castle. I don't think Cain could trace us. That second dream scared me. It felt like he'd found us. But he hadn't." Kai finished sheepishly.

"Are you sure your cousin won't be able to find us? Even after you accidentally sent that spell out." Maisie asked, as she swept the floor. Tiny particles of dust danced and twirled in the rays of sunlight which had found its way in through the air holes in the ceiling.

"As sure I can be about anything. I've learnt to never assume anything about him. Though I'm sure if he'd sensed us or followed us, we'd know about it by now. He's not subtle. He's impatient, he wants to win the war and steal all magic and power for himself." Kai bit into what looked like a giant peach, the sticky sweet juice ran down her chin.

"That's his vulnerability." Stella spoke, though she knew the wisdom to be Hecate's and not her own. "We saw his numbers, though we must assume he still has regiments out scouting for us. Most of the coven will be as obnoxious and self-serving as he is." She paused. "Though maybe, the children, those identified with the blue green light, aren't all as keen to follow him, as they appear to be. They may be waiting for the opportunity to escape. We may be able to use that to our advantage."

"There's something about a tattoo too." This time Stella's voice. "A tattoo with an arrow."

"Cain has a few tattoos. One in particular he likes to replicate on each of his coven, as a way to exert power and control." Kai confirmed. "I refused to let him mark me. The only time in our lives that I have won against him."

"Those tattoos, he uses them to brainwash the others, to keep them under his control." Stella continued.

A sudden rush of sound reached the room. As if the castle had suddenly filled with people. Stella and her friends piled into the hallway, as a crowd of people poured into the space in front of them. Most of the people she recognised from the market, though she couldn't put names to faces.

"Morning." Catherine bounced in as Stella and the others made way for the crowd. "These guys followed as we left Dumfries. They were keen to come and lend a hand and support us. I assured them there's room for everyone." She turned to the group behind her. "Find a seat, there's plenty of food and drink." She smiled at Brigid, as she came through the door to the larder, with two platters of breads and sweetmeats.

The benches in the tavern quickly filled. A head count confirmed around one hundred people had joined their cause. Half an hour later Stella and her friends served platters of food and tankards of mead to everyone.

"What do we do now?" Whispered Maisie.

"We need a leader." Brigid suggested. "Does anyone know where Broomhilda is?"

Flix popped his head up out of the pocket of Stella's coat. "Broomhilda's preoccupied with another task. Stella, why don't you address the group?" He asked. "All they expect is a few words welcoming them, making them feel at ease, it doesn't have to be a big speech. They did volunteer of their own free will." He reminded them.

From where she stood, Stella could see most of the group, their faces animated as they spoke to their acquaintances, making new friends, caught up in the excitement and anticipation. "Hi." She started. "Thank you for coming, for joining us." A hush rippled through the room as people stopped talking and turned to face her. "I'm Stella, this is Maisie, Brigid and Kai." She motioned to where Luna stood with her coven. "Some of you may know us, and Luna, Catherine and Tizzie. We'll be helping to train anyone who wants to learn about sword work, fighting, but also making spells and potions, using and growing herbs and plants for healing, and other skills we're going to need to win this war."

Kai moved to stand by Stella. "Unfortunately, it will come to war. I know Cain and his coven too well, but that will come in handy for us. They fight, with one goal – to win, yes, but to take magic and power from others."

A dozen tiny lights flew in the open doorway. Broomhilda landed on the top of the bar. "Echoing what Stella has already said, thank you, from the bottom of my heart. My friends here will show you to your quarters. There's plenty of room for everyone." She assured the crowd. "Take the day to settle in, while we work out the schedule." She nodded to Stella and the others. "There's always food and drink here for those who are hungry or thirsty."

As the crowd followed the tiny beams of light, Stella noticed it was their wings and their clothes emitting the beautiful, coloured lights. A smile crept on her face, as the fairies smiled and chatted to their charges as they led them to their quarters. She asked Broomhilda. "How many rooms are in this castle? How many floors high is it?"

"It's higher than it looks, and wider too." Was the mysterious answer. "It can reach up into the clouds if it needs to. You could say it's fit for purpose, centuries ago it was tiny by castle standards. This isn't its biggest iteration, but this is the largest group we've catered for in a long while." Broomhilda's aura shimmered, as if she'd been rejuvenated. Intuitively Stella understood her role as leader to support the oldest fairy, to ensure her continued good health.

"I don't think I've ever been in a castle, not in this life at least, yet this feels familiar. Like I've been here before." Stella, in awe of how the castle appeared to grow and morph into the shape and size as required, considered she may have lived here in another life.

"Hecate's been here before. This castle is part of your heritage. With Hecate's knowledge and Kai's understanding of how her cousin operates, you'll be the one to make sure we're safe. Review our defences, our walls, our protection, offer advice, and organisation. We need Hecate, through you Stella, to advise us how to keep the castle safe and protected. Kai, you'll assist, your knowledge of your cousin is invaluable." Broomhilda turned to Luna, anticipating her objections. "Luna, I understand why you don't yet trust Kai. Please work with Kai and Stella. You lived through a war, yes, I know we all did, but you learnt and lost so much, your instincts will keep us safe."

Luna stepped in place beside Stella. "Yes. Of course I will." She shot Kai a glance. "I'm willing to give you the benefit of the doubt." Her voice wavered as her eyes gave away her distrust, her fear.

Stella leant over and hugged Luna. "We're in this together. All we can do is try our best. I'm sure that if we work together and follow our instincts, we'll be okay." Her stomach felt like hundreds of butterflies were trying to burst out through her belly button. She pushed away thoughts of her children. They were safe, they couldn't be taken away or harmed. The spell she cast should protect them. Hopefully this would be resolved soon, and she could travel to visit them as she planned.

Chapter Fourteen

H ecate
Stella saw the castle as it was years ago. An army guarding the entrance, where a shimmering protection spell acted as a second layer barrier. The rainbow bubble, a giant version of those she used to blow through pipe cleaners with her children, so long ago. The guards wore the deepest navy hued metallic looking suits. Not armour, but not the robes of the marketplace. Their head coverings protected their heads, and ears, and blocked their facial features, except for piercing blue eyes. The turrets, full of members of the army, and under the protective orb, large birds guarded the fortress. Phoenix? Or some type of medieval eagle? People were travelling through the courtyard, along the turrets and through the building. Dressed in grey, others in a deep burgundy, suits, as with the army clothing, neither robes, nor armour. Stella couldn't name the material. It was scratchy between her fingers as she tucked her hands up the arms of the reddish coloured suit she was wearing.

A material nothing can penetrate or ruin

Hecates knowledge. She suspected this knowledge would guide her to the location of these garments, enough to clothe everyone in their castle.

The scene changed. She gazed at the castle from outside its walls. The structure barely visible, hidden by a thick layer of trees, bushes and a river that ran past, over rocks and branches. Old undergrowth and trees that reached up so high she couldn't make out where they stopped. At her feet their roots twisted and turned across the entrance to the castle and along its boundaries. The river wound its way in and out of these roots, stones, rocks, moss and bushes with thorns on them so big that they'd easily leave a gash in need of stitches. Other trees bore fruit and berries. Hecates voice warned her those weren't edible, unless she wanted a bout of gastrointestinal disease.

"This is how we cloak the castle, so it's visible to our people, but to everyone else, it's thick, dense forest. The tall trees, the river where the water is flowing so rapidly, and the thick prickly bushes?" She whispered, answering her own question.

Fae Magic. Creates the shimmer, illusion, weaves the magic that's real. Those with pure intent can enter. Safe.

"Do the fae create the other protection around the castle as well? The army and the strange birds I saw in the turrets?" From where she was standing, she couldn't see the turrets or even the sides of the castle walls.

Instead of Hecate, it was Broomhilda who responded. "Hecate is the strongest sorceress I know." Broomhilda replied. "Apart from the Fae, hers is the oldest magic alive. The birds you refer to are the phoenix. Many animals work with us, to protect the fae, and future generations. They're assisting Kai's coven with their school. Others will provide support here."

Stella found herself in a room she hadn't seen before. Two tables were lined with papers, and weapons. She recognised a bow and arrows, like something out of a show on television, and some knives, not for cooking, and swords. A shiver ran down her spine.

The ancient fairy was sitting in the middle of one of the tables, not phased that surrounding her were items that could kill her.

"The army I saw in my vision, Hecate's memory. Will our army come from those who've volunteered their time to help us, or can we conjure them from somewhere?" Stella was sure she knew the answer, but she hoped for an easy way to win this war.

"I'm afraid that we'll be training those who are willing to learn how to fight. There's no easy answer, and the fae will do what they can, but it's a human war. A battle of wits, and determination. A good versus evil, but without a predetermined ending. That doesn't mean you're on your own. Hecate will show you what you need to know. Use her knowledge and skills to make this a victory for good over evil."

Before Broomhilda finished speaking, the door slowly opened and Logan, Angus and Blair walked in. "We can help train the army. We've put the call out across the realms for volunteers. Many people are keen to help us defeat the coven. They should arrive in the next few days. Weapons are coming from the sea to the east. We've been promised herbs and spices, those that harm and heal." He looked down at his feet, then back up at the group in front of them.

"Logan has a habit of making friends wherever he goes." Blair grinned.

Logan blushed. "I can't help it if women find me irresistible." He mumbled.

"Having lots of friends might come in handy if we're to win this war." Stella suppressed the laughter in her voice. An image of an older woman chasing Logan away with a heavy pan, flashed in her mind's eye.

"What did we miss? Flix showed us where you were." Catherine spoke as she arrived with Kai, Luna, Tizzie, Brigid and Maisie. They squished shoulder to shoulder in the now crowded room. There were no human sized seats. Broomhilda didn't often entertain humans in her private office. If the others were surprised to see the fairy sitting in the midst of a pile of weapons, they didn't comment.

"Hecate shared with me, what this place looked like in the past. Broomhilda and I were discussing tactics, then Logan and his clan showed up. They were telling us about Logan's love life." Stella couldn't help giggling as another image, of Logan being chased out of a tavern flashed before her. She decided to save him further embarrassment and not mention the encounter. "Maybe we should get a battle plan together. We could start classes tomorrow. Years ago, when Hecate fought the coven, you were able to banish them for a longer time, but families were lost. Do you know what happened? Hecate hasn't shown me that yet." Stella asked.

Luna looked like she wanted to speak, but it was Broomhilda who responded. "It was a confusing time. We were so busy looking forward that we didn't properly protect those we needed to. We focused on beating the coven, instead of planning ahead, and making sure there were fail safes, and enchantments to protect the vulnerable. This time we'll do it differently."

"NONE OF THEM HAVE AN original thought." Cain complained miserably to Mabel. She ground the blade of her sword until it shone in the sunlight. She wasn't listening to the master, but he had no idea. His ego wouldn't entertain the thought that his followers didn't hang on his every word.

"I can't find any of them anywhere. Which means they must be tucked away together somewhere. Pretending they have a battle plan and preparing for a war they surely must know they won't win." It annoyed him. If he couldn't see them, how could he pretend to control the wayward women who kept attempting to banish him? Control of his coven, that didn't require any thought. The tattoos and the enchantments woven into their clothing kept them obedient and subdued, even Mabel, who he trusted as much as he trusted anyone, which wasn't much. They'd grown up, side by side. Bound together, soldiers in a war.

Little did he know. Mabel was biding her time. She considered herself the true leader of the coven.

Chapter Fifteen

Hecate
Stella's pulse pounded, her wrists, her chest, even that vein in her neck pulsed as she followed Hecate's footsteps. Each time her foot touched the cold stone floor, her toes tingled, her memories linked to her ancestor. Thankful to be wearing sneakers, not to be barefoot. The stone walls, the ground beneath her feet, felt as comfortable, familiar as her home back in Australia. The cold stone should have numbed her fingers, as she ran them along the walls. Instead, they warmed as she wandered the corridors, as if she belonged there, a part of the ancient sanctuary. Hecate beckoned her to explore the nooks, crannies, and hiding places that she'd visited before, in another time, as Hecate.

Her ears strained, voices whispering beyond the walls, conversations, words she couldn't make out. A gentle tap on her shoulder. Stella whisked around. A transparent figure beckoned her. A sense of urgency to hide. She slid into the space where two walls joined to turn the corridor east and watched as three ghostly figures walked where she'd stood a few seconds ago.

Visualising a rainbow stream of light wrap around her, keeping her safe, Stella left her hiding space, her heart pounding so loudly she was sure the apparitions would hear her approach. She followed them, until they walked right through the wall at the end of one of the unusually long corridors. Why was this area deserted? With hundreds of people joining the group, there should be more wandering the halls, getting the lie of the land.

Having not explored this far before, Stella back tracked, the hairs prickled on her neck, not danger, but an indication of some kind of magical being lurking nearby. She shook her shoulders, shaking the feeling of doom that was creeping around the edges of her consciousness. Now was not the time to fall apart.

Hearing voices, Stella moved towards the noise, seeking company after the strange afternoon. The space designated as tavern had grown since lunchtime, to accommodate their growing numbers. Each table laden with platters of food and tankards full of amber liquid. Most of the benches assigned to the tables were full. She smiled at those she recognised, and those who waved and smiled at her. Maisie waved, sliding up to make room. Stella slid in next to Maisie and Brigid. "Where did you go to?" Maisie asked, scrunching her face in concern for her friend.

Knowing that her face would be even more worried, but not willing to keep secrets from her coven she explained the strange occurrence. "I didn't feel threatened by the ghosts, if that's what they were. As Hecate I think I knew them. I may have been watching a scene from the past, part of Hecates life in this castle. Nothing outstanding or scary." As she tried to reassure her friends she was in no danger from her ancestor, Maisie frowned.

"I don't like you wandering around by yourself, anything could happen to you." Maisie's brow furrowed. Stella daren't comment that she wasn't alone with Hecate. That would've made matters worse. "You won't have any time to get lost in the past, for the rest of today, we have to prepare for war." Maisie gulped. "I mean prepare our training schedule; we start tomorrow." Even though the phrase – *prepare for war* – had everyone freaked out, they all knew it was a war they couldn't afford to lose.

Brigid passed a plate of cheese, bread and sweetmeat to Stella. "You should eat something. It's going to be a long evening." Stella smiled at her friend; the bread scratchy in her fingers as she broke it into pieces small enough to eat. She missed the food she ate at home but would never tell her friends here that their food sat heavy in her stomach. She swallowed the lump once her jaw hurt from chewing, wincing as it scratched her throat on the way.

Her third eye read the energy of the room. Animated, excited whispers amongst those seated with their family and friends, full of nervous energy, what would the next few days bring? Others sat quietly pondering the contents of their tankards. She didn't need to be a mind reader to know what was on everyone's mind. She should probably be a little more worried herself. It must be Hecate, making her brave, and excited to get this chapter underway, Stella normally hated confrontation. So much so that she didn't argue as much as she should have, to keep her children safe. No time for regrets, for Cain would certainly sense weakness. Not about to let another bully win, it was time to banish Cain and the Mark of the Thirteen once and for all.

At the table to her left, Kai attempted to strike up a conversation with Luna, with a smile she passed the tray of bread to the crone. Luna took a piece of bread, and without saying a word, she turned to Catherine and Tizzie. Before Stella could call out to her friends, the people in front of her changed.

The firmness of the seat under her dark blue robe, the newness of the wood of the table, the acrid smell of the food on the platter, Stella knew she was Hecate, her body held itself differently, straighter, her feet in open sandals, the leather straps wrapped around her legs a little uncomfortable. Across the room a much younger Kai, surrounded by youths of a similar age. Hecate wanted Stella to pay attention. The blonde lasses, sisters, if not twins, must be Penne and Sage. Stella recognised them from Kai's description of her friends. Hovering above the other teens, the blue green hue which she believed signified children stolen from their parents. Why did the youngsters look familiar? Scrunching her eyes, she debated crossing the floor to ask their names.

A hand on her arm, Stella gasped, as her bottom landed firmly on the seat nest to Maisie. "You zoned out, where did you go, and are you okay?" Maisie whispered.

Stella ran through the scene in her mind. "Hecate keeps showing me glimpses of her life. I think I'm supposed to figure out what's significant. Did I miss anything important?"

Brigid passed a tankard across the table towards her. Her nose twitched, the smell of roasted coffee beans, albeit magically sourced, focused her brain. The pounding ache near her third eye eased a little. "Tomorrow morning training begins. Everyone's volunteered their time, so they choose whether they learn sword work, invisibility, or the other skills. The fae have arranged space for us to teach, they'll show us after breakfast tomorrow." Brigid drank deeply from her tankard. "We should all get an early night, though I'm not sure I'm tired enough yet."

"I know what you mean. I'm going to stay up for a while." Stella placed her hand gently on Maisie's. "Please don't worry about me, I'm fine. We're all going to be exhausted and full of nervous energy. I will tell you Hecate's messages, when I figure them out. No secrets. Let's not give Cain any leverage to separate us."

Many of those who'd occupied seats for a while were huddled together, chatting quietly. She watched as others stood and waved as they headed outside or maybe to their rooms. Catherine stood by the doorway, wishing everyone a good night's sleep ahead of a full day's training the next day. Numbers in the tavern dwindled.

"We're going for a walk outside, to cast a spell by the moon, for success for our plans." Catherine whispered to Brigid. "I'll take the first shift tomorrow morning if you like."

"Sounds good to me." Brigid agreed. "Tomorrow evening it might be our turn, depending on how the day pans out." Tizzie and Catherine waved as they followed Luna out the door.

Stella took the opportunity to speak to Kai, joining her at the table, on the seat recently vacated by Luna. Kai was stacking plates, and tankards to return to the kitchen area. Most of the inhabitants of the castle were happy to pitch in and help, rather than leaving it to any one group to do all the work. Stella placed the last plate on top of the pile ready to go to the kitchen. She spoke softly. "Where were you the last time, and how old were you and your friends?"

"You mean when Luna fought The Coven?" Kai's face turned grey, like she was going to throw up. Her hands shook as she dropped the tankards she'd stacked to one side, the cups bounced off each other as they clattered the few inches back to the table.

"Sorry, I startled you, it mustn't be a great memory, but yes. Hecate shows me visions, and I'm trying to work out the timeline." Stella spoke gently, but firmly. "To gather as much information as I can."

"I attended a school for the children who belonged to the coven, children from the village attended too, if their parents worked at the castle or for the coven in some way. The school closed; I don't think I ever knew why. Lessons were conducted at the castle, coven members taught us math, literature, and spell work, combat skills too. I hated it, and I left a couple of years later, as soon as I was old enough."

"Where did the other children who attended the school go, when it was closed down?" Stella was curious.

"That's the thing, I never saw any of them again, apart from Penne and Sage, who came back to the castle with me." She looked down at her hands. "I've been thinking about this, and the thing is, I think this is when he started taking the children. Before I was sent back home, new children started to arrive at school. Those with no magic, from other realms." Kai's voice was little more than a whisper.

Stella's stomach tightened; a lump formed in her throat. "I saw a vision, as Hecate. You were at school, at a long table with some other children. I got the distinct impression they were Luna's." her voice little more than a whisper, her mind whirling as she worked it out. "I saw another vision a few days ago, the same children, living in an orphanage, I think. Someone called their names, the same names as Luna's children. I didn't know whether to tell her. Now I've seen them twice I must be meant to." Stella paused, considering whether she should ask the next question. She lowered her voice a little, though no one was paying them any attention. "What happens to the children he takes?"

Kai's eyes widened as she realised the implication of what Stella was saying. "He keeps them in a school, an orphanage, and brainwashes them, so that the coven is the only place they want to be. Some leave the coven when they are old enough to, others stay as part of the coven. Some disappear. I always thought they left of their own choice, but then again Cain's never happy if anyone disobeys him or disagrees with his plans. I've never been brave enough to think that through properly."

"You're the bravest person I know Kai. You help rescue children at great cost to yourself." Stella stood up, picking up as many plates as she could carry without her hands shaking, and headed towards the kitchen. Kai followed, a pile of tankards in her arms. Maisie took the plates from Stella's hands, placing them in a large copper pot filled with boiling water.

Brigid held out her hands for the tankards, shooing both women away when they attempted to wash the tankards. "We've got this covered, you too are deep in conversation, it'll be your turn next time."

A few people remained behind in the tavern. Kai spoke softly, as Stella followed her over to a quiet spot near the fire. "On my last night at school, I remember a conversation that made no sense. My cousin was talking to a man I didn't know. One of the parents, I thought at the time, because new children came and went all the time, some stayed, but others disappeared after a few days. They discussed a family of four children, giving them new names and relocating them somewhere far away. I haven't thought about this for years. I remember though, wondering why they got to go somewhere exciting, and I had to go back home. I wished I could be part of their family, then I'd have a brother and three sisters. They were nice, not pretentious like those who thought they deserved a place at the school, these kids were different, I asked my cousin about them as I thought we could become friends, but he told me they'd moved a long way away."

"I don't suppose you remember their names?" Stella asked, hopefully, aware that it was a long time ago. Her heart broke a little more each time she thought of what happened to Luna. It wasn't that different from her own circumstances. Not all evil doers had magic running through their veins.

"I think the oldest girl was Anne or Annie."

Stella gasped. "I think one of Luna's children's names was Anne. I'm pretty sure she had a boy and three girls. I remember, because I also have three girls and a boy."

"Do we tell Luna?" Kai asked.

"Tell Luna what?" Flix stuck his head out of Stella's coat pocket.

Chapter Sixteen

Luna
    Could it be true? Did Stella and the new witch Kai work out where her children might be? Her stomach twisted, as if a rope was tying it up in knots. Could her grown up children be alive and safe somewhere, with no memory of her or who they really were? With no recollection of their lives as young children?

"I don't know whether to be happy they're alive or devastated that they have no idea about me." She told Catherine and Tizzie. The flames danced in front of the three friends as they gazed into the embers. Light emanating from the full moon cast weird shadows through the trees. Luna threw a handful of basil and bay leaves into the fire, taking a deep breath as the smell reached her.

"It's time for celebrating that we finally know they're alive." Catherine leant over and placed a hand on Luna's. "I'm convinced you'll be reunited with them one day. For now, let's bask in the gift of the full moon."

Broomhilda's castle garden had many peaceful nooks. The grounds grew and changed depending on the needs of those living there at the time. "It's peaceful, our own moon festival, just the three of us." Tizzie wrapped a thick blanket around Luna's shoulders. The three ladies snuggled together, under the blanket, on a log near the fire.

"How clever of Stella and Kai to piece together the story of the children who were taken." Catherine gazed up at the sky, full of stars. "I know you don't trust her, but even Flix believes that Kai is doing her best to help us defeat Cain." The three sat in silence, grateful for the message Flix had delivered, that Luna's children were likely still alive, and that Stella and Kai would do their best to find them.

Luna broke the silence. "If anyone's able to find a way to reverse the spell, for my children to remember who they are, it'd be Stella."

"Stella's a powerful witch on her own." Tizzie agreed. "With Hecate's memories, her magic is stronger, controlled, fearless. We may not yet trust Kai, but I've the feeling she's on our side." The moonlight shone on the three women. Luna tilted her face, so her cheeks bathed in the light of the moon goddess. Her fingers and toes tingled, as they often did when she spent time outside. Her affinity with the seasons, and mother nature, her muscles and joints tightened and flexed aligned with natures heartbeats.

"We must find them, all the missing children, so Stella can reverse the enchantment that's kept them captive. I know, we should be focusing on how to defeat Cain and his coven first. Cain must consider Stella a threat, he went to such lengths, kidnapping her to remove her from this realm." Luna's confidence returned, her voice was stronger, steadier, at the thought she might see her children one day after all.

Catherine stood up, warming her back against the fire. "I think it's linked somehow. Kai joining us, finding out your children are alive, Stella and Hecate's combined power. The solution, our victory, will be linked too. By defeating Cain once and for all, we free our loved ones."

Luna held one of her bony, worn, garden-stained fingers to her lips. She pointed over to the high castle wall with another. As the three women stared, they saw three tiny figures, nimbly drop from the wall, landing about fifty metres away from them.

As the beings ran closer, Tizzie whispered. "Has The Coven coerced the elves to do their spying?" Her friends didn't answer. Catherine stepped closer to the elves to intercept them. Luna was feeling on the ground for a stick, her fingers grasping at leaves and twigs. All three kept their eyes on the elves. Dressed in shades of brown, cloth that appeared to be made from leaves, bark and mud, sewn together with the tiniest of stitches, the creatures ran quickly, low to the ground. Closer to the height of the mice who lived in the garden around the castle, rather than Jinx, the castle cat. Luckily for these three, Jinx loved nothing more than to spend hours curled up in front of the fire in one of the rooms.

"Eww, no respectable elf would work for Cain, no matter what he was offering or threatening." The heavier set of the three spoke up as they reached the fire. Luna remembered reading somewhere that elves had super clear hearing, able to hear a leaf fall in the woods miles away from where they lived. She'd thought that an exaggeration. Until now.

"We thought we'd perform some recognisance for you lot." The second elf said gruffly. "Our hearing after all is far superior. We could hear the goings on with The Coven, without having to enter the castle walls." A sobering thought for anyone who thought elves were harmless, or of no consequence. It made a lot more sense why some families employed them as castle sentries.

"You'll need strength in numbers." The heavy-set elf continued. "Their numbers increase daily. More than a hundred, maybe two, follow him, or are committed to him, the master's a way of making people do his bidding."

"We should be telling Broomhilda this." The smallest of the three reminded the others. "She'll want to know what we found."

As if on cue, a slight fluttering of the air nears Luna's ear, signalled the fairies arrival. "Faelyn, Fylson, and Feirn, it's good to see you. Would you like some food and somewhere warm to stay? You're always welcome in our castle."

"Thank you, but we must be getting back to our clan, after we tell you what we've discovered. The Coven numbers at least a couple of hundred. All loyal, or bound to Cain, to do his bidding." Fylson, the largest elf retold the story for Broomhilda's benefit.

"Mabel's teaching everyone how to fight. It's mandatory in that castle, for everyone to learn everything – war skills, enchantments, and potion making." Feirn, taller, but not as heavy as his brother, spoke. "No one complained about the training, as we'd expect from a large group. As if they were under some kind of spell."

"That makes sense with what Kai's told us." Luna nodded. As she watched the elves more closely, she noted a family resemblance, beyond the pointy ears that elves were commonly known for. Their eyes, the shapes of their faces. Not having spent much time with elves, their size, colouring and lyrical tone was fascinating.

The youngest, and the smallest of the siblings spoke. The strength in her voice told Luna that Faelyn was someone not to be underestimated. "They're planning to attack within days. Cain is furious that you've all disappeared. He's directing his army to search this area until they stumble through your enchantment."

"That could take them ages." Tizzie said.

"They couldn't accidentally find it straight away, could they?" Luna was alarmed at that idea. Her heart thumping so loudly she dreaded it would give away their location.

A cloud moved in front of the full moon, covering the group huddled around the embers in an eerie shadow. Luna shivered. A ghostly finger ran its ancient finger down her spine. She resisted the urge to swing around, no one behind her, the otherworldly touch a reminder of lost loved ones from beyond the grave. The full moon the time when her friends tapped her, reassuring her they watched over her. Friends from so long ago, missed every single day she remained on this earth. A shiver of anticipation ran down her spine, tracing the line left by the ghostly fingerprint. Rather than alarming, the spooky interaction calmed her beating heart.

"He can probably guess the rough area, but no, Cain won't be able to find the castle. It's more likely that he'll try and goad us to leaving the castle, then he can attack." Broomhilda's voice wavered, the challenge of constant fight mode wearing on her energy. "We need to grow our numbers, to encourage people to join our cause. I don't say that lightly, and I don't mean coercing anyone." She lifted her head, letting her shoulders drop a little, faking the confidence, shaken, as they were facing Cain for a third time in under a year. Twenty-seven years to recover and regroup behind attacks; reasonable, this ongoing onslaught was not.

"A lot of our customers from town are keen to help, but they don't want to move here, to disrupt their lives. This place isn't for them." Catherine said quietly.

"What if some of us taught the townsfolk how to defend themselves?" Tizzie asked. "Although that would open them up to an attack from The Coven."

"There might be a way." Broomhilda mused. She gave Faelyn and his siblings a meaningful look. Cain wasn't looking for elvin magic, their presence in the village would likely go undetected.

With a glance and a shrug, the elves nodded at each other. "I guess we could help with that. After we check on our family." Fylson acknowledged, a small sigh escaping his lips. "We'll be in touch."

Luna watched as the three elves nimbly ran up and over the castle wall, disappearing within seconds. "I wish my old legs worked that well." Luna shook her legs, under her black skirts and her leggings, wincing as her knees creaked and cracked, reminding her of her years in this realm. She laughed to herself.

As the embers died down, Luna, and her friends joined Broomhilda as she headed back to the warmth of the castle. The crone listened as her friends spoke, her thoughts were with her children, last seen so many years ago. Would she recognise them? Their voices? How tall would they be? How had they spent the last twenty plus years? Here or in another realm? Another world?

"I believe Kai's one of our biggest assets in this war." Catherine said. "Cain's army is growing significantly. We can hope for increasing numbers in our group, but we need Kai's skills and knowledge of The Coven to ensure when we fight, we defeat them. Permanently."

"Kai, Stella and Hecate. Those stories of bairns taken from their beds, ripped away from their families is true – we know that now. Those three women will defeat The Coven and rescue those who were taken." Tizzie wrapped her arms around Luna, who leant in, feeling safe and loved.

"We can win this." Luna meant it. "We can re-unite all the children he took with their families and break that spell of evil he's cast on so many. "I think you're right. That Kai, Stella, and Hecate are key to our success." Luna scuffed her shoes on the cobblestones in the courtyard as they moved back into the castle.

"I had a brother." Catherine said quietly. "A wee bairn snatched from his bed. He's the reason I insisted we needed a school, to teach magic to those of us left behind."

"I knew about your brother, although you didn't tell us. The names of those taken from us are whispered in corners of the village, keeping their memories alive. We've all suffered the loss of someone. My cousin and I the same age, we used to spend most days playing in the forest together." Tizzie said. "When she vanished, my parents told us not to speak of those who were taken, instead we were to honour them quietly as we go about our business. But I think we got it wrong." Her voice got louder. "I think we're meant to speak and yell their names at the top of our voices to remember them and call them home."

Catherine, Tizzie and Luna followed Broomhilda to a smaller room, with chairs near the open fire. The women sat, while the fairy perched on the edge of the table. Luna balanced on the edge of the chair, her feet firmly on the floor, worried if she lay back in the plush chair made from deep brown wood and beautiful blue material, she'd fall asleep. Her toes wiggled, she flexed and wiggled her feet, energy flowing through her extremities, excited at the thought of seeing her family soon. After all these years. She blinked and focused on her friends. Catherine and Tizzie sat back in their chairs, all eyes were on Broomhilda.

"I suggest we call a town meeting, tell the towns people, honestly, what we know. We offer training, for those who don't want to relocate to the castle, we can offer them elvin training, or offer to transport them here and back each day, from the village square. The focus must be on winning this war. The rest will fall into place. Now let's get some sleep, we can update the others in the morning." She flew over to the fire, turning around, letting the heat warm her aching bones. "Relax, spend some time together. I think tomorrow's going to be a busy day."

LUNA FELT A PIECE OF the puzzle was missing. Something nagging, just out of view of her third eye, warning *caution*.

If Stella and Kai were telling the truth. and she believed they wouldn't lie to her, then her children had their memories wiped, creating new personas for them. Did that mean their father and grandparents had also been given new names? Or weren't they involved in their disappearance after all? A vein above Luna's eyes pounded. It was too much, to think that people she'd once known and trusted had gone to such lengths to remove her children, but what if they'd no choice? She always thought they were involved but now maybe not. She shook her head to clear the cobwebs. No! They were involved – she felt it down to her very core, why else would she have been unable to find any trace of them when she returned from the war.

"It wasn't your fault." Catherine whispered from her bed. The three had chosen to share a room, to look after each other. "You were called to help fight the war, to keep the world safe. You thought he'd care for them and protect them until your return. Sleep now."

THE MARK OF THE THIRTEEN had been removing children from their homes for over twenty years. The master took as much delight in this now as when he'd begun, by taking Luna's children away. Mabel shook her head, as she polished the blade of her sword.

Things will be different when I take over. She thought to herself. She'd learnt the art of encrypting her thoughts on one of her trips to the orient. *Military school for all the children in the realm. From the age of five.* The master would never agree to it. Luckily Mabel had a plan to remove Cain. All she needed was for Stella and Kai to win this war.

Chapter Seventeen

Broomhilda

She'd stopped counting birthdays so many years ago. The fairy who was arguably the oldest being in the realm, didn't remember her own age. Her friend, the ancient yew tree, with her roots spread far underneath the river that ran past so close to her enormous trunk was older, by quite a few years. She knew of no other creature, flora or fauna, older than her. Her sister Gertrude, significantly younger, but fae weren't obsessed with age or birthdays the way that humans were.

Broomhilda's head pounded as she flew out of the castle and over the market town. Nothing looked out of place, those who chose to stay were getting on with life. "It'll be interesting to see how many are interested in working with us." She said to her sister, flying at her side. The older sister always wore dark colours, none of the sparkly colours for her. In contrast, the younger sister loved bright colours and the more glitter the better. Today she was more subdued, convinced by her sister that they needed to blend in rather than stand out, in her favourite green dress, without the sparkles.

"Catherine will report back this evening." Gertrude tried to calm her sister. She knew the sign of an approaching headache. "I'm sure the townsfolk will be happy to help us."

"We're asking a little more than mere assistance." The older sister said tartly. "I'm sorry, I know you didn't have to come with me this morning. I appreciate you being here." She flew lower, over the market square. Her sister followed, marvelling at the colours in the array of materials at some of the stalls.

People gathered in the middle of the square, supporting the stall holders, now back trading after the fire. "Let's leave this to Catherine and her sisters."

Gertrude said gently. "Stella and Kai started the training this morning, there's no need for us to return straight away."

"What do you suggest?" Broomhilda was curious, her sister wasn't normally outspoken.

"Why don't we visit the fairy glen? I know it's your sanctuary." Gertrude didn't normally take the time to stop and smell the flowers or sit and reflect on life under the trees welcoming branches.

Broomhilda appreciated the effort. "I do yearn for peace, and time with my friend, the ancient tree. I love the colourful flowers, the gentle spiky leaves, the thicker hairy ones, all part of the delicate balance of the magic that's even older than I. Even an ancient being like myself gets exhausted around too many other creatures." Broomhilda lay her head against one of the soft feathery leaves at the base of the tree. "I'm feeling the emotions and auras of everyone, humans, fae and other enchanted folk. Everyone is on edge, worried or ready to fight. I didn't put my protection on fully as I wanted to see what was going on. A decision I regret now."

The tree sat silently, while her fairy friend processed what was happening in the world. The tree had witnessed many wars and much disturbance. This time it was different. Many people were unintentionally allowing their true colours to shine through.

Gertrude wandered away, giving her sister the chance to talk to her friend in privacy. The vibrant colours of some of the flowers were intriguing. She was keen to create a range of clothing to capture the energy of nature's creations.

"It's stronger than normal, the emotions and the longings of the population. I'm not the only one tired of the struggles between good and evil." Broomhilda's team normally advised her of any problems. "I wanted to see for myself if that feeling deep down in my gut was true." She sighed – a sigh far bigger than her size. "I wonder how long this has been brewing. I like to think I'm normally on top of this sort of stuff. I did let it all slide, thinking that we'd banished the coven for a few years at least."

At least now she knew. It was impossible to do nothing. Nor was it possible to keep the malevolence at bay. Confirmation that she'd made the right choice, to make preparations for war.

"I was surprised to discover that most people are prepared to step outside of their comfort zone and tackle the evil head on, not wait to be attacked and then retaliate." She flew up to the very top of the ancient tree's branches. From here she could see where the realm morphed into another. So far away, the tree so tall she saw the void where most magic folk stayed well clear of unless their intent was less than worthy.

Gertrude found her sister, followed her gaze and knew instinctively what was on her mind. "Surely you don't think his evil could reach here, this glen is sacred, and it's already protected and hidden from malevolence."

"I don't want to take any chances." Broomhilda held her arms aloft, muttering words known only to the oldest of fae. A spell to cloak and keep safe the whole fae realm, all the fairies and elves she had charge of, their land and where they worked and lived. Her enchantment joined with the glow of the protection spell she set years ago, strengthening the thread that kept them safe. Gertrude shared her energy with her sister, strengthening the intent and the power of the spell.

Ancient magic, so old it wasn't written in any books, save for the hieroglyphs etched in places known only to the most aged magical creatures. Magic to hide the clearing, the fae and other innocents from Cain and his crew.

"Will the same spell afford the same level of protection for everyone in the castle?" Gertrude whispered. "I know it's hidden and protected, but the energy of so many humans in one spot, does that affect it?"

"I've the same concerns sister. I've spoken to Stella and Kai. They'll ensure the safety of the castle and its inhabitants. Stella trusts Kai, and so do I. Hecate's appearance is an added bonus. We may be able to win this war." She sighed as she flew back down to the bottom of the tree. She lay her hand on her roots, "I'll be back my friend. We'll see this through."

The sisters parted ways as they returned to the castle. "I'm here whenever you need me." Gertrude assured her older sibling. Both had rooms in the castle; the younger sister was keen to change into something with more glitter.

BROOMHILDA'S WORKSHOP was as small as the bottom drawer on a dresser, except that it was four metres tall and with shelves and floors in a higgly piggly fashion along two walls. Her workbench ran the length of one wall, the other held a large chimney for the open fireplace at the bottom. With her cauldron hanging in the fireplace above the embers, Broomhilda lit the fire. Sparks hissed and shot out tiny embers, as all magical fires do. The flames coloured blue, green, purple, orange, yellow and of course red. A fire for magic, and warmth as well.

She tossed in bay leaves, citrus peel, aniseed, herb roots and leaves and some ingredients from jars passed down through the ages. Amber jars so old the layer of dirt was darker than the glass. The fire popped and sparks flew up and out in various directions through the open window. Bushes and trees sprung up across the pumpkin farmer's land. As she watched, the bushes grew thicker, entwining around each other and the farm gates and living fences. Trees shot up, growing taller with each passing minute. For miles around the castle all that could be seen was forest. The raging river, that started somewhere up in the hills, swept along the ground where seconds ago potatoes had grown. A mass of birds chirping, insects scurrying, and tiny woodland creatures scampered as if they had always been there.

"Not a bad illusion if I do say so." Broomhilda admired the woods which while she called them an illusion, to any passersby the trees were as real as the castle hiding behind it, and as old as the rest of the lands around it.

Inspired by the image that Stella described when she'd stood at the castle gates the previous day, Broomhilda wove a protection spell, strengthening the existing enchantment. The rest was up to Stella, and Kai. She flew back in the window of her workshop, a window too small for anyone else to find. Her workshop hidden in the middle of a maze at a place in the castle, impossible to locate, without an invitation.

Her younger sister wasn't the slightest bit interested in her collection of books, jars of herbs and potions that sat along the shelves. Sometimes the oldest fairy wished she had an heir to hand down her knowledge to. Other times she didn't want to burden anyone with such responsibility. There were fairies who would take on the role if she asked. Flix, or others in his line. She hoped to pass on the baton during a time of peace, with time to teach and guide the next in line, not hurriedly in the middle of a war.

As she was contemplating the various fairies she could trust, a crow flew up to the window and sat on the ledge. A crow. An omen.

A wave of energy buffeted the castle, knocking the crow off the ledge. Cries of surprise sounded from the grounds and from the rooms behind her workshop. She flew quickly through the corridor to the tavern. Designated the general meeting area, it was rapidly filling with people, others spilling out into the courtyard which sprung up along one wall, to accommodate the increasing number of inhabitants. Anxiety levels were high, cries of shock, anger, concern and fear filled the air. She watched in horror as another shock wave whooshed through the space.

From the middle of the room a counter wave repelled out, sending the previous shocks back out to the perpetrator. As the energy reached the edges of the castle, it added an extra layer of defence. Broomhilda felt it. She braced herself for more, but nothing happened.

"Stay calm everyone. Cain is sending out those waves randomly, trying to locate our hiding place. I'll wager he'll leave without having discovered our location. All he can see if he looks directly at our fortress will be a wood that's hundreds of years old." The crowd quietened, most taking a seat at one of the tables, waiting to see what happened next. As Stella spoke, the fairy recognised Hecate. For the first time in a while she believed they had a chance to beat the malevolent master. Not send him into hiding for a few months or exile him for a year; to rid the realm of his evil forever.

THE HOODED ONE STRODE away and jumped up on his horse. He must be mistaken. This woodland was clearly thousands of years old. He pried a splinter out of his thumb, wincing as it scratched his skin. "The fairy must be mumbling, jumbling the aura, creating confusion so I search in all the wrong spots. It's like they've vanished." He muttered as he climbed back on Bolt, his black stallion steed. He yanked the reins, causing Bolt's neck to involuntarily swing in that direction. Cain paid no attention to the emotions of his horse as he galloped him hard, back to his castle "They can't hide forever." He told his steed. Neither creature believed his words.

Chapter Eighteen

K^{ai} Kai liked a clear, strong knowledge of her surroundings. Broomhilda's castle morphed and moved in response to the number of people inside its walls and their requirements. Being accepted by the powerful fairy, and invited to the fairy glen and then to join the others in the castle, an honour she didn't take lightly. She'd feel more at ease if she understood the lay of the land, so to speak. Eager to fight alongside them, against her cousin, after she worked out where this corridor led. "If I was Luna, I wouldn't trust me either." Kai confided to Flix. When the first shock wave hit, Kai and the sprite went room to room, making sure no one was injured. "I swear the rooms keep moving around, have we checked this room already? Broomhilda must trust Stella, to have me stay here."

"Stella told the fairy that she trusted you, and so did I." The sprite confirmed. "When I first saw you, in that car park, watching Stella, I sensed you weren't a threat, but I didn't tell Stella. Broomhilda wanted me to watch over her. I'll never forget that morning, when Stella made you a cuppa and a sandwich and marched over to meet you."

Kai nodded. "I was stuck, with no choice but to do Cain's bidding, until I found a way out from under his clutches. I'm forever in her debt for helping me escape." She pushed open a door that looked like every other door, solid wood with metal fixing. "How many rooms are there in this place?"

"Several hundred, though we don't have to check them all. Only seventy-nine are being used although that number changes each day." Flix said. "Even I don't know where all the corridors lead to, or how to find all the rooms. Have you noticed the corridors lead us to where they need us to go?"

"Yes! I thought I was imagining that." The room was empty, like all the others. The next door she opened, took them back to the dining hall. She looked at Flix, who shrugged.

"Our best defence against Cain is to train, to plan and defeat him." Stella addressed the crowd, as platters of food and tankards of mead were delivered to the tables by a dozen fairies. "Let's eat now and spend the rest of the day preparing our attack. He may keep trying to locate us, but it's unlikely that he'll succeed. The castle will keep bouncing his energy back, confusing him. He'll lose track of where he's already searched."

Without much of an appetite, Kai excused herself. She felt nauseous, sensing her cousin searching for her. Refusing to give in, she blocked him, pushing his energy away, sending him instead to search for her in Brisbane, that part of the world where she'd first met Stella. As far from him as she could travel. She hoped he might believe that she'd stay away, to keep him permanently away from her friends and the children.

Another option, she hesitated to think of, to return to The Coven and pretend to be his ally. It worked once, but could she pull it off again? She'd pleaded for him to believe they'd kidnapped her and placed her under some spell. His ego was large enough that she may get away with it. She shuddered.

"What's wrong?" She twisted around, Stella's voice dragging her from her thoughts. Kai turned, tempted to reply that nothing was wrong, but this was Stella. Or maybe Hecate, both were powerful. She didn't want to lie to either of them. "Cain is trying to get into my head, to find us. I was concentrating on sending him as far away as possible, back to where I first met you. I shuddered, as I considered whether I should go back. Trick him, convince him that I'm on his side and bring back what I learn to you. I couldn't bear the thought of it."

Stella hugged her friend. "No one expects you to go back there, no matter what information you may be able to glean from him. Use your strengths here, teaching us what you know."

Kai nodded. "I can help train the others to recognise The Covens energy, their tricks and to recognise the signs if they're nearby. I trained with Mabel, an expert in the art of war."

"Do you think there's anyone else here who used to belong to his coven? Or still part of his coven, spying on us to report back to him?" Stella enquired, as a group led by Tizzie were practising their cloaking spells in the middle of the courtyard. In the arbour, Catherine showed another group how to use their hands to manipulate the energy around them. Too busy concentrating on their craft, no one paid any attention to Kai and Stella.

Kai considered the question. It wouldn't be easy for one of Cain's henchmen to get through the enchantments, specifically set to block any with malevolent intent. The problem with brainwashing followers would leave them vulnerable away from their leader. "I can't see any coloured orbs, or any inkling of his energy, nothing to suggest he's infiltrated our fortress. We've put such strong protection around the castle. I'll keep an eye out for anything that feels like it doesn't belong. Do you mind if I visit my coven, for a couple of hours, to make sure they're safe. He was looking for me here. I don't think he can find them, but still..." Kai couldn't bear the thought of anything horrible happening to her friends or the children.

"Of course. We can manage here, but I'd like you to show us some of his tricks, later this afternoon, if you're up for it." Stella replied.

Before Kai could leave to visit her coven, the castle gates swung open and shut again, the metal sides clanging together, heralding visitors. She recognised Logan and his crew as they halted their horses right in front of them. "That was a blast!" Logan's face was flushed. "Galloping our horses full pelt towards the river and the woods, knowing the castle was there, but not being able to see it."

"We thought he was crazy." Angus agreed. "But we'd follow him anywhere. So here we are." The younger of the three said, his voice full of the excitement of racing a horse through a magic doorway.

"We can't stay long this time." Logan's voice was still a little breathless. "A day ago we discovered Cain's army. We were cloaked so they didn't see us. They were making preparations to destroy the portals to the other realms, to stop us escaping or seeking aid from other lands. I happen to know someone who breeds dragons." He blushed as his younger cousins made kissy noises, squishing his lips against the back of his hand. "Anyway, we got to the portals first and there are dragons guarding each of the entrances. His army won't be ruining the portals or escaping through them."

"He'd hate that. My cousin believed he'd banished the Goddess Marta and her dragons. He boasted of how dragons were extinct, because of him." Kai frowned. "He'll be furious, he hates to be made a fool of."

"He's more than dragons to be worried about." Logan laughed. "Mabel plans to rule The Coven. There's talk that she'll deliberately lose this war, so she can defeat Cain in a bid for leadership." He climbed down from his horse, leading it over to the water trough by the side entrance to the castle garden. His cousins followed, their horses eagerly lapping up the water.

"Logan wants to make friends with Mabel, to see what's she's up to." Blair laughed, as his younger brother made the same noises on his hand.

"That's not true at all." Logan frowned at his charges. "I have my sources. We're due to meet at a tavern on the other side of the realm, where some of the army stay when they're deployed. It's amazing what you learn when you have something to barter." Logan waved his hand with a flourish and a shower of jewels and coins bounced onto the ground.

Kai watched, fascinated as the heavy gold coins bounced, twirled and lay still on the ground. Red stones, blue stones and green ones, bounced over the coins, nestling near them. The youngest one scooped the spoils up, tucking them into a velvet pouch.

"Logan has a knack of conjuring up what is desired. A family gift, his family were often mistaken for thieves, which they're not." Stella said firmly. "Hecate." She added, as Logan raised his eyebrows.

"I've a question and don't take this the wrong way." Logan addressed Kai, who nodded, for him to continue. "Would you go back to your cousin, to attempt to gain valuable intel?" Logan's question didn't appear to bear any malice. "I'm not trying to send you away or get you hurt or anything." Logan added hastily. "It'd be good to see how the rest of the coven feels."

"I've thought about it. I'd do that as a last resort. If we've exhausted other avenues for gaining information. I know he trains the army to fight with swords and their fists, but also with enchantments. Blurring the lines and confusing their opponents. I've shown Brigid how, she's going to train our army. We'll know what to look for and how to defend and attack."

"If Mabel is planning to lose this war to get rid of Cain, we mightn't need to worry so much about tactics." Logan reminded them.

"Unless Mabel is then planning to continue with his plan and steal magic and power for herself. She's a mean and angry woman." Kai shuddered, realising how much she enjoyed and valued her life away from the negativity of the coven she'd been born into.

"Standing around talking won't get us answers." Logan jumped back on his horse, his cousins followed suit, each patting their animals, whispering words of encouragement in their ears. "I'll send back word when we learn more." Before Kai or Stella could say anything else, they watched as the horses and their riders galloped back through the gate, which slammed firmly shut as they did so.

And then Kai went back to her coven.

Chapter Nineteen

Stella

The castle bustled with energy. If Stella read the sun dial correctly it was early in the morning. Brigid and Maisie were already out training a group of the more enthusiastic residents. "Sword work, potions and invisibility." Hecate, through Stella, requested the three most important skills at this stage in the war. Like having a sister or a cousin, living in the same body, Hecate wasn't bossy, or parent like to Stella, she manifested more as self-confidence, and an awareness of things she'd once known, and was re-learning. The gaps, the lack of knowledge about the moon phases, the witch celebrations, she remembered it all, along with the knowledge of the spells Hecate cast over centuries. Her innate intuition and ability to move through portals and to manipulate energy and the elements grew stronger each day.

"After breakfast, could you take a group in the opposite direction, and practice divination and casting enchantments?" She asked Catherine. The old Stella would have felt uncomfortable delegating tasks.

"I am taking a group out to practise what we've learnt over the last few days." Catherine agreed. "I think we're ready, but we won't know until we're face to face with them."

"It's the waiting that's difficult." Tizzie agreed. "I want to stay with Luna, if that suits you, Stella. "We want to make sure we have all the medicines ready, in case of injuries, or worse." Tizzie whispered, there were stragglers finishing their break-fast feast. She quickly collected the remaining platters, piling them on the bench near the larder, ready to be taken out and cleaned up, in preparation for the next meal.

"I agree. It's like waiting for any ordeal to be over. I want it done so I can get on with my life. To spend time with Maisie and Brigid, then see my children.

Are we prepared? How do we decide whether we wait longer, or take the fight to him? That's the question." Stella left the tavern, in search of Broomhilda. Instead, she found herself in another part of the castle. She watched Luna setting her potions along the table, scribbling a label for each describing the ingredients and the ailment it eased.

Lavender – burns and boils, Peppermint – fevers and stomach issues, Oregano – warts, Tea tree – skin irritations, frankincense – maladies, The aromas of the potions filled the apothecary. Stella could quite easily stay there all day, amongst the herbs, oils, potions, and lotions.

"Are we doing the right thing? Fighting this war using force? Should we instead be using magic? Our magic, rather than physical attacks?" She asked Luna, the affinity these women shared, as healers filled her with hope for a peaceful outcome. Neither woman appreciated raised voices or conflict of any kind, though both would stand up to defend those they loved.

"It has to be both I think." Luna said "But I'm not the right person to ask. I lost everything and I'm still fighting for that, yet at the same time refusing to fight. It's like I'm being torn in two." She shrugged, holding her palms out, a gesture of openness, of friendship.

"I understand that. Hecate's in my head, and I understand the need for war. To demonstrate force and strength, to win and banish the evil. Yet that goes against who I've been. I lost my kids, because I wasn't strong enough to stand up to their father and his family. They took my children, I couldn't fight, and I lost the opportunity to bring them up with peace and calm and love, in a life with no drama. It annoys me that I'm still this soft woman, ready to banish the coven, without the courage to physically attack." Hot angry tears trickled down Stella's cheeks. She ignored them, letting them sting her cheeks and her lips as she spoke.

"I think it takes courage to not fight. I can't forgive or turn the other cheek; I say I'd fight whoever took my children, but I'd probably scream and cry and throw things in a tantrum, rather than a considered, planned attack." Luna's tears ran freely, as they'd done so often before. "I run and hide, or I rant, then run and hide. I yell and I cry. My emotions are my undoing. I'm not fierce enough, or coherent enough to command respect." Luna scribbled some more jar labels, her ink pen writing a flowery script the words *chamomile – calming, feverfew – headaches,*

"I think you've created the persona of a crazy witch woman so that you aren't asked to make any decisions. You didn't lose your children. They were taken from you. Kai and I can't promise, but we'll do our best to find them." Stella's hand hovered over her friend's arm, not wanting to encroach on the crone's space, but wanting her to know she was loved, that someone understood, that hidden part of her.

Luna nodded. "You're correct. Acting like a crazy woman lets me get close to people, they ignore me, thinking they can speak freely in front of me. I've learnt so much by acting like the crazy lady." She grinned, and Stella realised that under that exterior, the women were also closer in age than she'd realised.

"There's got to be a way." Stella focused back on the problem facing them. How to win the war. "We could cast a spell that spreads throughout the land, directing it to only affect the coven of malevolence." Stella said, thinking it through. "We can cause rains, storms, fires and even droughts if we want to."

Luna nodded. "Manipulating the elements, harnessing the magic of nature and the seasons. It's still destructive but we aren't spreading a virus that injures or kills innocents. We can target those whose hearts are filled with evil intent." She dropped her pen on the table. Her gait was so wobbly, she tripped over her own feet as she took the three steps to where her *Book of Spells* sat on the bench. "Aha! Here it is." She pointed her arthritis ridden finger to a page titled *Messing with Meteorology*. "The teacher in me – alliteration helped me remember and find the spells when I needed them." She shrugged.

"What a great idea." Stella smiled. "I'm a teacher too, or at least I used to be." She flicked through one of the other books laying on the counter. "Ideally, we could cast a spell, causing them to fall into a deep sleep for hundreds of years, and banish them. But banishment and exile hasn't worked so well."

"Listen to us. We're both crazy." Luna laughed, "Ridiculous, that we still wish not to cause harm, but none of Cain's cronies would hesitate to end our lives."

Stella plonked down on the wooden seat alongside the long table. Days of no sleep affected her more than she was willing to admit. It was exhausting, being in such close proximity of so many others. "It's not in our nature, as healers, to fight to injure or maim but we know from experience that anything less than that and he escapes and evil wins." Stella knew Hecate was strong, determined and ready to win. Still, she wasn't hell bent on bloodshed as a solution. "Even Hecate would accept a peaceful solution, it just doesn't look like there is one."

"As long as I've been involved in this fight, we've reacted to a situation. When Cain, his coven, caused illness, or stole magic, we stepped in. The key this time, is whatever we do, we must act first. To have Cain on the back step for once. If we annoy him enough, he'll make mistakes." Luna spoke, as she shuffled the bottles of potions around on the table. Stella watched Luna's hands, as she deftly rearranged the bottles, so their labels ran in alphabetical order of ingredients.

Stella considered what Luna suggested. "That makes a lot of sense. Our next step is to talk to Broomhilda and get messages out to all our teams. You're amazing Luna!" Stella reached over and hugged the old crone.

CAIN SHIVERED. A BREEZE wrapped around his legs; his muscles tightened as the cold air clung on. Clammy, his long robes provided no protection against it. He spun around, expecting to see a shadow or a spectre playing with him, but nothing was there. The cold reached down, touching the bottom of his feet, sending a wave of ice through his body.

Hecate. It had to be! He swiped at the invisible tendril, in an attempt to free himself. He wasn't successful, the cold clutched at his stomach, sending another shiver through his body. No one else would be brave enough, or foolish enough to mess with him. He fell on the floor of his room. The cold cobblestones added to the dilemma the master found himself in. His pride stopped him from calling for help. His body ached, with the last ounce of his strength he stared at the fire, willing the embers to light, filling the room with warmth. After what felt like hours, his limbs numb, a tiny ember started smouldering.

Chapter Twenty

L una
    Crowds. The crones least favourite place to be. Tonight, it was necessary. To eat, to meet, and plan the next attack.

"He's convinced it's Hecate who caused the cold. It's hit him hard. The fire caught hold just in time." Flix reported to the group that consisted of Luna, Stella and their respective covens, Broomhilda, and Kai. A distant cousin of his lived not far from the castle and heard what happened from one of the guards, who was talking up big in the local tavern. "The guard was boasting that he knew something that would change the course of this war, that Hecate wasn't the only one that the master should be wary of. He implied it was someone within the ranks. He didn't go so far as to name anyone."

The cold had been Brigid's idea. A spell to grip Cain, to freeze him on the spot. "I can't wait to assault him with something else." She said with glee. "Not that I'm normally malicious, but he deserves it." She handed a tray of tankards around the group. Mead for the others, and a special coffee for Stella.

"Maybe it's not so bad here after all." Luna whispered to Tizzie, as they sipped their drinks. She leant back on her friends' shoulder, images of her children flashed in front of her. As she imagined them to be now. Freddie, Annie, Lizzie and Katie. "It feels so real, like I could reach out and touch them." She told Catherine.

"Whoa, hang on. Are we sure Cain isn't trying to mess with you, to drag you off on a wild goose chase after your kids?" Catherine sat up.

"I'm not going to do anything silly, like wander off looking for them." Luna said. Not having thought it a possibility anyway. "I've waited this long. A few more weeks until we win this war and free all the children isn't too long to wait."

Luna felt the eyes of her friends on her, concerned that she might wander off in search of her kin. It was tempting, but no, she'd wait. She'd promised.

"Tonight, as he sleeps, let's tie him up with some ancient vines. He'll wake in a panic that a snake is choking him." Tizzie suggested, rubbing her hands together.

"Won't he have tightened the enchantment, to keep us out?" Maisie asked, balancing platters of sweetmeats, breads, and cheese in her hands. Each table laden with platters piled high with foods, tankards in front of those seated. Other townsfolk who'd joined them in the castle, were in the larder, helping to prepare and serve the meals, or serving drinks at the bar with Brigid. They preferred to keep busy, and Catherine and Brigid appreciated the assistance.

"Yes, but his enchantment won't work." Stella said. "He thinks it's Hecate who's causing the harm. He's focusing his intentions in the wrong direction." Her newfound confidence continued to surprise her. She shivered, her skin damp with sweat, not that she doubted Hecate's knowledge, but if she was wrong...she shuddered. "Let's meet together later, when it's quieter, under the moon."

Once everyone had enough to eat, the number of people in the dining hall dwindled. It was Stella and her coven's turn to sit under the moon. "It's as if there's no one else around for miles." Maisie commented softly, as the three women piled sticks and twigs on the fire. The crackle and hiss of the flames cast its own spell, calming and strengthening the bonds of friendship.

"At last, we are celebrating the full moon together, as a coven." Brigid whispered. A ripple of energy ran through the clearing, each woman sensed it, and quite literally saw it. "With everything that's happening, we didn't have time to prepare anything for this occasion. I don't think we had to, seeing that." The women watched, mesmerised by the multi coloured lights that wove its way in and out of the trees at the edge of the clearing. Soft music, faint, as if from far away, wafted over the group, gathered around the fire, and the scent of rose and jasmine filled the air. "Fairy song." Brigid whispered, seeing Stella raise her eyebrows. The women sat, arm in arm, silently, not wanting to break the spell.

THE MOON HUNG HIGHER in the sky when Tizzie, Catherine and Luna joined them. "Do we need Kai here for this?" Catherine asked.

"I've travelled with Kai to the castle, not to mention I was there as Hecate, so let's leave her to spend time with her friends, it is the full moon after all." Stella could already see, through her third eye, where they needed to be. "If we hold hands, I can lead us. Tizzie, you're still happy to cast the spell?" Tizzie nodded. "I'm certain this is safe, but we're only staying there long enough to cast the spell. Keep our hands together, here, the whole time." Even as Stella finished speaking the six women found themselves in Cain's quarters watching the coven leader as he drank from a tankard on a tray on the floor where he sat, reading from a book. Tizzie wove strong vines, as thick as her arms, anchored beyond the floor and the walls, they crept over every inch of Cain, closing tightly over his arms and legs. Pinned to the ground, the more he struggled, the vines drew tighter, strangling him. A hiss from the window, as an adder whose body, twice as wide as the vines, slithered over to Kai's cousin, who tried to scream, but no sound came from his mouth. His wide bulging eyes, the sweat forming on his brow, Stella heard the sounds of fear, she smelt it in the air and saw it as his face drained of colour. It would be so easy to continue, until all the life was drained from this monster, Hecate's desire to finish him nearly overrode Stella's commonsense. Focusing on the clearing, where they'd begun, she drew them away, back to safety.

"It would have been easy, to finish him there." Catherine broke the silence. "We all wanted to."

Stella nodded. "That wasn't what we discussed, and I didn't want to make that decision for us. We have to decide that together." The women nodded, no one willing to speak the thought plaguing them all – *Would they get another chance to rid the world of this evil?*

LUNA'S EYELIDS DROOPED for the tenth time since their return from their adventure. "If nobody minds, I'm going to bed, it's been a long day." She hugged Catherine and Tizzie.

"We'll be there soon." Catherine and Tizzie waved as Luna ambled towards the castle. Her legs ached, as they sometimes did on days when she'd been standing for a long time. Her bed was comfy. She didn't bother taking off any layers, she pulled the blanket up around her neck and closed her eyes. Every muscle creaked and cricked, slowly untangling after standing and sitting, her bones and joints finding their spot. Her eyes closed, mantras running through her head. *Calming, peaceful...happy endings...being enough*

She was relaxed, floating on a cloud, until she rolled over and fell out of bed with a thud. Her eyes flew open, blinking as her brain caught up with what she saw. It wasn't the cobblestone castle floor. The ground beneath her was made of wood. Dark, in a confined space. Claustrophobic. Something grabbed her arms behind her. She swung her arms around frantically to free herself. A blanket fell on her. Not a blanket. A coat. Her coat, from the cupboard in her cottage. She shoved the coat away. Luna's eyes became accustomed to the dark. The shoes, the clothes hanging on coat hangers, she recognised them - hers.

Tentatively she opened the door, peering out to see if anyone stood waiting on the other side. Like the young lady Anne, who Luna had rented the house to. The old crone had imagined this Anne to be her Anne from so long ago. Now that she knew Cain had stolen her children, changed their names and moved them away, any resemblance between the lovely young lady and her children were shadows she'd been jumping at, looking for happy endings.

The bedroom was empty. As was the living area. Luna tiptoed, as nimbly and quickly as was possible for her, through her favourite room in her little cottage. No time to look around or reminisce, she wanted to escape before being found. Once outside, there were many hiding places amongst the garden she'd lovingly created, she paused to look back at the little house she'd made her own, in a secluded part of outback Australia. Far enough from any big cities or towns, the closest village far enough away that Luna kept a car. Not that she climbed into the old jalopy much. She preferred a solitary existence and grew or made most things she needed. A forest of sorts, bushland at least, at the edge of her garden.

The cottage looked the same as if she'd been there the day before instead of six months ago. Salem, a kitten when she'd left, now an adolescent cat. He jumped out from under the old rickety wicker rocking chair where he'd been observing her and ran over to the old crone. He wound himself around her black leggings. Her back made an ominous clicking sound as she bent to pick him up. Arthritis, old age, years of bending down to tend the garden. Luna ignored the twinge of pain as she scooped him up and cuddled him. Salem nestled into his witch, as he always did. Time stood still. His purring soothed her soul.

She remembered where she was. Home. But someone else's home, temporarily while she'd reason to be in the other realm. Anne, who rented her cottage was likely at work or university. Luna recalled the young lady wanted to rent the cottage so she could write a book. She'd not thought of her home for a while, to save her emotions and to keep the important facts about the war with the coven in her head. Too many thoughts and some are bound to fall out. Was Anne still putting money in the account for rent? She lost track, she didn't need to use the money with her coven. She'd stashed her bank card somewhere safe. She scratched her head, searching for the answer to reveal her hidey hole. "No matter, I'll remember when I need to." She crooned to her familiar. Her arms were numb, holding him for so long. She didn't mind.

"Cooee, is anyone here?" she called out in the general direction of the open door. Was it open when she'd arrived? Should she close it? "Let's check out the back garden." Luna placed Salem on the ground, to let the circulation return to her arms. "There must be a good reason why I'm here." She told him, "I love visiting with you and I'll probably be home for good once we banish the evil." The problem was, she loved her cottage and never wanted to leave, but the same thing happened when in medieval Dumfries, with her coven. Very annoying that she couldn't be in two places at once.

Luna wandered the path she'd built; through the garden she'd created from the dry crumbly dirt that she'd been faced with when the cottage called to her. Now, native trees and bushes stood tall, creating shade and a canopy for the smaller, more delicate plants. Autumn in the outback, yet still her flowers bloomed, fragrant herbs beckoned to her. She ran her fingers lovingly through the flower heads of lavender and rosemary, inhaling the aromas that calmed her soul. Her mood shifted, as she crushed a few mint leaves, inhaling as the essential oils coated her fingertips. Instant clarity.

"Cain didn't send me here, to get rid of me. If he wanted to mess with Stella, he'd be more direct." Dead heading the geraniums, she sprinkled the spent petals through the garden. Even the geranium's pungent perfume increased her focus. "This isn't about my kids either; now that I know they're safe and that

Kai and Stella will do their best to bring them home." Salem followed behind his witch's ankles.

In the back corner, where the black wooden fence palings met, stood a eucalyptus tree over a hundred years old, judging by its size. Old in this country's terms, a mere spring chicken back in the old country. Planted in front of the tree stood three rose bushes, thriving, thorny and full of spent buds. "No time to dead head these today." Luna murmured. To the left of these plants sat a nondescript metal box, an old lunchbox or toolbox maybe. Peeling black paint revealed it was originally a dark grey metal. Opening the box with fingers that didn't work as well as they used to, she fumbled as she picked up a pair of gardening gloves. In contrast to the tattered condition of the metal box and most of the garden tools hidden in her garden, these gloves looked new. Sturdy synthetic material, created to withstand rose thorns and other dangers of the garden. "Careful little guy, remember you can't follow me here." Salem sat obediently on the grass side of the roses, while the crone opened the latch of what had started life as a chook pen. Repurposed into a greenhouse, hidden at the back of sharp spiky plants that yelled a warning to any trespassers to *keep clear*. Whenever Luna stumbled across poisonous herbs growing in anywhere near where she lived, she took a cutting, carefully, and cultivated them, just in case. She'd never discovered a reason to use them, until now.

"This is why I fell through the wardrobe and came to visit." She whispered to the jimson weed, the belladonna, and the morning glory, as she carefully took pieces of the poisonous plants. "If only I'd thought to bring a bag..." her voice trailed off as she looked around her growing house. In the bright green plastic tub, amongst the little black pots and paddle pop sticks, was a screwed-up plastic zip lock bag. "Aha!" She held it up triumphantly. "Perfect." With fat gloved fingers she poked the herbs, that would cause hallucinogenic symptoms, or worse, if too much was used, into the bag. Luna squeezed the bag shut, stopping as she heard the click that signified the bag sealed.

Stepping carefully out of the hothouse, she shut the door firmly. "To make sure you and any other inquisitive creatures stay safe." The witch told her cat as she placed the gloves back into the metal box. The bag safely in one of the pockets of her robes, she picked up her cat and hugged him. "I'll be back soon. I promise."

The tree in the middle of the garden, one that dropped acorns from time to time, beckoned. "Will you let me through please?" She asked it. A little acorn, complete with its tiny hat, dropped into her open hand. She pressed it into the knot in the tree that curiously looked exactly like the tree fruit she held in her hand. A shimmery light appeared on the trunk in front of her. She closed her eyes and walked through the light.

She opened her eyes as Catherine and Tizzie entered the room they shared in the castle. Too tired to tell them of her adventures, she closed her eyes. Tomorrow would be time enough to share her idea.

Chapter Twenty One

Broomhilda

The jolt of the energy field reverberated throughout the castle. Unauthorised use of a portal to move between worlds. Broomhilda looked up from her journal. Writing a list of the tasks she needed to hand to someone? Should she be concerned that a portal opened in her castle, without her knowledge? Normally, yes, but her intuition told her no, it wasn't a threat from outside, but still...She sighed as she lay the pen on her book, waving her hand over her desk, hiding it from sight. Closing her eyes, she focused on the portal. She found herself in the room Luna shared with her coven.

"We were worried, when we couldn't find you!" Tizzic wiggled her finger at her friend, standing over Luna, who yawned and rubbed the grit from her eyes.

"Stella and Kai are searching the castle for you." Catherine further admonished her, though she sat on the bed, with a reassuring arm on her friend's blanket.

"We're here now." Stella and Kai crowded into the room. "We felt the portal open."

Luna looked suitably sheepish; her lopsided smile didn't stop her friends looking cross. "I didn't leave on purpose, but in my garden, in the cottage, I've been growing some herbs, poisonous plants. I figured we could use them in a spell to confuse Cain, to make him hallucinate."

"We could've asked the travellers to bring us some. They've offered to help us however they can." Stella gently reminded her.

"That'll take time." She said defensively. "Anyway, I didn't deliberately open the first portal. As I nodded off to sleep, I fell out of bed and through the portal in the wardrobe. I did open the portal in the tree, to return." Luna added.

"It's done now. No harm done that I can see." Stella patted Luna on the arm. "Does anyone want a drink, to settle our nerves?"

An idea, at the back of her mind, taking shape, keen to test her theory, Broomhilda followed the group to the tavern, though she wasn't thirsty. With every cell of her body, she knew it was no longer her place to lead. The strongest fairy found herself at a crossroads. She yearned to spend her days at the fairy glen with the tree and watch nature pass by. That wasn't possible, whilst others considered her their leader.

"I was thinking, we could use the herbs to confuse Cain. Cause hallucinations and make him mad. Crazy I mean, not angry. Does anyone else think it will work?" Luna picked up a cloth and fished the plastic bag out of her robes. She deposited it on the highest shelf behind the bar.

Stella held her hands out, moving them ever so slightly, and the plastic bag disappeared. The group gasped. "I've moved it somewhere safe, in a locked box in our apothecary." She told Luna. "We can cast the spell first thing tomorrow. I'm expecting an update from our friend who knows the guard. He'll be drinking at the pub near the castle again this evening. Flix promised another update at sunrise."

Brigid passed out tankards. "Mead for everyone, but coffee for you Stella. How long have you been able to make objects move?"

"Thanks for the coffee. I've never done that before, first time luck." She shrugged it off.

Broomhilda nodded to herself. Her tiny heartbeat so fast in her body that her wings fluttered quickly. She caught Flix watching her from the pocket of Stella's coat. She poked her tongue out at him. He grinned in return.

"By eight tomorrow morning, we'll have cast the spell to send Cain into a spin. He won't know who to trust, or where to turn. He'll see creatures that don't exist and lash out in all the wrong places." Stella said, with a confidence that came from her ancestor. "Luna, Kai, please meet me at our apothecary before the sun rises, so we can get all the ingredients prepared."

A few minutes later everyone retired for the evening.

In the short distance to her rooms, Broomhilda knew the time had arrived to hand over to Stella. The interaction in the tavern confirmed it. This fairy made excuses, delayed the inevitable for long enough. She didn't need to write lists, Stella, even without Hecate, knew what needed to be done. Instinct, from centuries and past lives as healer, as a powerful magic woman.

Stella couldn't find Broomhilda anywhere. She'd hoped to check in to make sure their idea to turn Cain mad was sound, with no negative repercussions.

"You know Broomhilda trusts you." Flix climbed out of the pocket and sat next to Stella on the stone floor outside the fairy's rooms. "If she can't be found it means she agrees with your plan and is leaving you to get on with it." The sprite, having worked with Broomhilda for a few years, sensed the change in the oldest fairy's actions. Broomhilda was stepping aside and letting Stella take charge. "You mightn't see her for a while. That normally means she knows she doesn't have to interfere; she trusts that others, in this case – you – have the situation under control."

Stella considered this. She wasn't sure she placed as much confidence in herself as the others did, but it was time for action.

HE RUBBED HIS HANDS together. Mabel informed the master that the coven of do gooders were fighting amongst themselves. He'd no reason to suspect Mabel wanted to take control and fed him misinformation to make him believe he didn't have to work hard to win this war. His ego did the rest. He addressed the coven during their evening meal. "It's come to my attention that the group we're up against, are fighting amongst themselves. The leader has disappeared, one of the crones, has crossed into another world, and some of the others are travelling in other realms. There is no show of strength, we can defeat them in a few days." Cain puffed out his chest and smirked at the crowd of eager servants.

Chapter Twenty Two

K^ai The visit to the castle had been an accident. Maybe she'd been curious and wanted to figure out for herself how bad things were in the place where she'd spent most of her childhood. Not that she felt anything other than contempt for her cousin. Mabel, as awful as Cain, wily, strong, determined, but did she intend to steal magic from others?

People were gathered at the tables in the dining hall, food platters nearly empty, tankards and jugs of mead passed between the group. "The master keeps talking in riddles about goodies and ghouls and spirits who are attacking him. Mabel is hard on us when we train, but she doesn't talk nonsense the rest of the time." A man older than Kai, she recognised from her time in the castle, spoke. Others around the table, leaned in, nodding in agreement.

His nosy sister agreed. "We don't need someone who gets sidetracked by ghosts. Mabel will make sure we're safe and have all we need."

"What about the masters plan to take all the magic and power?" The younger blonde man asked.

The woman sitting next to him, with dark hair, pulled up into a ponytail, shoved him onto the ground. "Are you stupid?" she laughed. "He's no intention of sharing any of it with anyone. He'll likely kill us or throw us out of his castle once he has what he needs."

Kai would have felt sorry for her cousin. If he hadn't been evil and mean his whole life. Good riddance.

CAIN TOSSED AND TURNED in his sleep. Something wasn't right, but his conscious mind wouldn't hear a word of it. When he was awake, he was the exalted leader. During slumber, his long-repressed intuition was trying to warn him of the threats. Mabel and his coven working against him. He didn't know that they hated him, his greed and his ego wouldn't let him entertain that thought. His coven was ready for a change. It wasn't Stella and her coven that were falling apart, it was his very own henchmen that were actively working against him.

BY THE TIME SHE'D RETURNED from spying on her cousin, she found Stella and Luna in the apothecary. While it was dark, the full moon lit their way to the herb garden. "Fresh herbs work as well as dried, for some spells." Luna told the others. "I like using dried bay leaves, but fresh lavender and rosemary. The herbs I brought over yesterday are still fresh enough."

"Normally I would have thought a potion like this, that we'd have to get him to ingest it, to have it work effectively." Kai said. "How will this work if we enact it from here?"

Stella reached out and took both women by their hands. "I've been thinking about that. It would be extremely potent if Cain was to drink it himself. How we do that, I'm not sure."

Kai bit her bottom lip. She cringed at the metal taste in her mouth. "I've an idea. He always has his first meal of the day in his quarters. While he sleeps the servants take a plate of food and drink to his room, so it's there when he wakes. He doesn't wake before eight, normally, so if we can get it to the castle, I'll pour it into his morning brew."

Luna frowned, her fingers playing with the pages of the book open in front of her. The book of spells listed all the ingredients for the enchantment, and the instructions were easier than she thought. Stella frowned too. "I don't like the idea of you going there, it's dangerous if you're caught."

"If I don't the enchantment mightn't work as well. You know that. Come too if you like. The same way we travelled last night, though I'm not sure I can hold hands and pour the liquid at the same time. We can be in and out quickly."

"Here." Luna shoved a small bottle into Kai's hand. "It's done. Don't touch the liquid yourself. It's very strong." Luna didn't see the need in telling them she'd doubled the quantities of belladonna, morning glory and jimson weed. As long as they didn't let it touch their skin, they'd be fine. She rubbed the spot on her hand where one small drop had landed. She was already loopy, so everyone thought. She could ride this out, and everything would go back to normal. The crone sat on the floor, crossed her legs and opened a book on her lap. Upside down, the book. She bent her head, reading the words that strangely made more sense than normal. She chuckled.

"Is she alright?" Kai asked Stella.

"Did you spill a drop on your hand?" Stella called out to Luna.

Luna looked up and shook her head. "My finger." She held her hand up. "I'll be fine, I'll sit here and ride it out, I'll talk to the stripy cat and the green bat, and everything will be fine."

Stella fished Flix out of the pocket of her coat. "Go find Catherine, and Brigid. Tell them what we're doing and ask for someone to sit with Luna. I promise we'll be back soon." Flix, waggled his finger and opened his mouth as if he wanted to say something. He changed his mind, nodded and disappeared.

"Come on." Kai reached for Stella's hand. They both closed their eyes and focused. Opening them a few seconds later they were outside Cain's quarters. A young servant girl was placing the tray in front of his door. Kai held her finger up to her lips motioning for the girl not to speak. The young lass placed her hand over her mouth to stop herself gasp. Wide eyed, she nodded and ran quickly back towards the kitchen. Kai bent, tipping the contents of the bottle into the tankard. The liquid hissed and bubbled, changing colour from dark brown to a lighter hue. Unlikely her cousin would notice the subtle change.

Kai's shoulders clenched under the heavy fabric of Stella's invisibility cloak draped over both women, at the same instant the door to Cain's quarter opened. Her cousin's eyes darted around, peering along the corridor. He sniffed the air, squinted, staring at the spot where they stood, picked up the tray, retreated into his room and slammed the door.

She turned so she was facing Stella. "Thanks for the invisibility cloak. Perfect timing." She whispered. "Let's stay and listen, to make sure he drinks it." Stella nodded.

"Help! Fire! Dragons! Get out of here, you beast! Wait, no don't eat all my food. No! Not the plans to win the war too!" A loud bang accompanied Cain's raving. Another bang and a third. A couple of guards entered the corridor, running towards the commotion. Kai and Stella joined hands, focused on Luna and the safety of their castle.

Chapter Twenty Three

As the sun blinked over the horizon, the dining hall buzzed with people preparing for their lessons, as the ringing in her ears from Cain's tirade slowly subsided. Stella spoke loudly, to capture their attention. "Before you leave, we have an update for you." The eyes of everyone in the room turned towards Stella and Kai.

"Early this morning we added a little something to Cain's drink. A simple spell, that will cause him to see things that aren't there. Hallucinations. He'll slowly lose his grip on reality." Stella projected her voice, ensuring it reached everyone in the hall. "We have it on good authority that Mabel is going to let us win the war anyway, to drive him mad, and then fight him for the leadership of the coven. Not that we can count on or believe in her plan to save us. We're ensuring the success of our own strategy."

Kai nodded her head. "Mabel is mean, she's a military person, it'll go against all her principles to throw the fight. We haven't yet confirmed if she's also after our magic, but I think not. Her interest will lie in building up their defences and their fortress."

Before anyone could ask questions, the door banged open, and a small creature appeared. "Excuse me!" A gruff voice piped up from the back of the crowd. "Where's Broomhilda? I've information she'll need to know." Most of those gathered swung around to find the owner of the voice. A heavy-set elf, whose red pants hung down a little too low, revealing a matching pair of under garments, waved his hand in the air. The sleeves of his orange shirt were too short, it looked like his clothes had shrunk in the wash. Or in a clothes dryer. Stella remembered the time she'd accidentally shrunk some nice tops she owned by leaving them in the dryer for too long.

"Broomhilda's busy. She left me in charge." While that technically wasn't true, she decided that someone had to be, and she was pretty sure no one else would fight her for the position. Or was it Hecate in charge? These days she couldn't tell where her ancestor's knowledge stopped and hers began. "What information do you have?" Stella's voice carried over the crowd. Something told her she could trust this elf though she hadn't seen the creature before. He'd been allowed to pass through the fae enchantment, so he must have important news to share.

He strode up close to Stella. Eyeing a bench not far away he leapt up more nimbly than Stella thought possible for an elf of his weight, until they were almost face to face. "There are clock towers, that cross the world and the realms, a little like the lay lines in your land and ours. The elfin book of magical fables talks of these old landmarks as holding a dark banishing spell." He paused. "These structures don't appear to be anything special, when they lie dormant as they have for hundreds of years. Crumbling, dilapidated, in need of repair, in ruins some of them. In the last few days, the energy around them has changed. There's a humming heard by animals and magical beings, elves and the fae. The teachings in our books talk of having to harness the energy, when it awakens, to banish a great evil, elsewise the evil will use the energy to banish all good in the world." The elf hopped onto the table closest to him and grabbed a piece of sweet bread almost as big as he. He sat next to it, tore a piece off it and munched on it.

A murmuring ran through the crowd. Panic rose in the room, the anxiety of the gathering contagious. Stella held out her hands, calming the energy. A faint light emanated from her fingertips, weaving through the room, lightly touching the anxious ones. The noise died down, as the anxiety eased. Silence filled the space as people turned to her expectantly.

"Is that all the information you have for us? Do you know the locations of these clock towers? How long do we have to act, before the towers explode? Do you know the spell to banish the malevolent?" She spoke to the elf, as he munched on his third piece of bread. Would her voice carry the power and authority elves, fae and other enchanted folk expected from Broomhilda.

"Yeah." The elf tried to sound like he didn't care but Stella heard past that. She heard the disappointment in his voice. "All our books have vanished. We think the coven hid them or stole them. Some of us are old enough to remember the stories but none of us have visited the places or cast those spells." He stepped back and tripped over his own laces, which were tangled in some crumbs from his breakfast. His cheeks reddened. Stella reached across and helped him to his feet.

"I remember the spell." One of Broomhilda's fairies hopped up onto the table, eyed the elf suspiciously and edged closer to Stella. "Years ago, Broomhilda required the details of that spell and the locations of the clock towers. I used to scribe for her. I have a very good memory. I remember the locations of five of the clock towers. There is one, in your world, near where you live when you don't live here. The banishing spell is written in our ancient book." Swift, that was the fairies name, Stella remembered, because she'd noticed her bright blue and pink hair the first time they'd met at the fairy glen.

"If we were able to find the towers and cast the banishing spell at those locations, we could banish the coven for good? Is there a guarantee it'll work better than last time?" Catherine called out from where she stood with Luna and the others.

"I think it will, if I take part in the enchantment. I suspect I'm the missing piece that will contribute to the effectiveness of the spell. As I once belonged to that world, that coven, by family ancestry, though not by choice." Kai moved to stand with Stella.

Stella gauged the mood of the crowd. She'd been so focused on the conversation she hadn't noticed that more fairies and elves had appeared. She recognised the faces as belonging to the council, from the fairy glen. The fairies and elves were talking in hushed voices. The humans in the room were more vocal.

"Do we trust her?" Logan called out, pointing to Kai. "She tricked Cain once; how do we know she's not tricking us now? We've travelled through from the other realms, and the energy levels near the portals are very unusual. It adds weight to what the elf said."

"My name is Bonce." The portly elf said huffily, not bothering to stand up. He was busy nibbling away at a piece of cheese.

"I trust Kai." Stella's voice was firm. "I've no doubt Kai would give her life if it meant The Coven would be stopped, as would any of us." The crowd stopped talking and stared at Stella and Kai. Something in Stella's voice commanded silence. "Broomhilda has entrusted me to lead us to victory over the coven.

I want to ask for two days. We've prepared to fight, but if there's a way that doesn't require losing good people, I think we should try that first. If I'm not able to stop Cain before sunset tomorrow, someone else can lead." There was a gasp from the crowd. Heads turned, to see if anyone would challenge Stella. "I trust Kai. She despises Cain as much as we do. I want Kai by my side in this war."

Kai stood silently beside Stella. She'd give her life if it meant her cousin would never lay a hand on any other living being. Stella heard her thoughts and squeezed her hand.

"I'm in." Luna stood beside Kai. "I know in the past, I've been critical of Kai, but I was wrong. She's proven herself an ally." She tucked her arm in Kai's. "We must be as crafty as Cain. He thinks he's won. He thinks we're at each other's throats, fighting and bickering and that our army is failing. I saw him watching us a few days ago, when we were in the village. I acted like I was a little more loopy than normal, muttering to myself and dancing around, he paid me no attention. I heard him telling one of his cronies that he had us fighting each other and he would win."

"Clever." Logan conceded. "We could've quite easily gone down that path, each of us thinking we were right and everyone else was wrong. Let our ego's get the better of us."

"When we disappeared, he thought we'd gone away, our own separate ways. He's too self-centred to imagine that we could be as coordinated as he thinks he is. Broomhilda's magic is too strong for him to penetrate. I sent him on a wild goose chase to the other world. He thinks I've run away." Kai's cheeks reddened, as the crowd leant in to listen to her words.

"You'd never run away from a fight." Stella said. "We know Mabel is trying to take over. We've cast a spell and given Cain a potion, to drive him crazy. Now we know about the clock towers, that changes things." Her head spun. So much information, so many options and ways this could go. In days their plans changed from physical combat, to poisoning and driving him mad and now sending him and his coven away for good. If this is what being a leader is all about, no wonder Broomhilda needed a break.

"When we leave the castle to find the clock towers and cast the spell, will Cain and Mabel be able to trace our actions?" Brigid asked. Somewhere in the castle a clock chimed nine times, indicating the day lay out in front of them, full of possibilities. Stella hadn't slept much, and the early hour surprised her. A couple of people shuffled their feet. Luna's legs ached from standing still for a long time.

Stella noticed the restlessness in the room and moved to sit on the bench closest to her. Slowly, the others followed, she waited until everyone was seated. "Cain and Mabel won't know where we are, until we get to the towers and activate them. We'll have a small amount of time, no more than a couple of hours. Hopefully that'll be enough."

Swift, the fairy who'd mentioned the enchantment returned to the table where Stella was sitting. "My sisters and I, seven of us, are willing to meet people at the clock towers, with everything you'll need to cast the spell. We can set everything up. Cain and Mabel won't be looking for fae magic." She handed a small slip of paper to Stella. "The locations of the clock towers."

"The elves can cause a ruckus to distract them, if any of The Coven get suspicious." Bonce said gruffly. "They're still scared of us. Some of my cousins play practical pranks on them. Cain falls for it every time, but because he's a megalomaniac he refuses to acknowledge it. It makes him mad."

"When he's mad, he makes mistakes." Kai confirmed.

Stella bent closer to her new friends. "Thank you, both of you. Broomhilda would be proud of how strong and brave you both are."

Bonce's cheeks matched the shade of the tomato like fruit on the platter to his left. He bowed to Stella. "Anything else you need, just holler." He muttered to her, alighting from the table and disappearing into the crowd.

Swift curtsied. "Elves don't understand praise." She explained. "My sisters and I will make the preparations." Before Stella could respond, the fairy flew over the heads of the crowd.

"I've protected my aura and my energy from my cousins prying. If he tries to find me, he'll fail. That'll make him even crazier." Kai added.

Luna put her hand up, to talk, while an idea hit her. "The fairy book provides all the words and ingredients we need for the enchantment. In one of the books in the apothecary there's a spell for keeping our mind clear and focused and hidden from anyone with less than pure intent." The old crone nodded to herself. She put her hand on Kai's and spoke more softly this time. "I think you're right Kai. You're the missing piece. When you join with us, speaking the words to banish the coven, your energy will ensure its success."

"You can count me in." Kai said quietly. She turned to Stella. "Are you willing to lead us?"

Her heart pounded, thumping as the blood coursed through her body. Sweat glistened on her palms. Her body tingled as if someone was tapdancing on her grave. If this failed, she'd likely never see her kids again, but it she did nothing the outcome may be the same. "Yes." Stella didn't hesitate. "If the majority are happy to try the banishment, before bloodshed. If there's a way not to lose anyone, I'd prefer that option."

"Count me in too." One by one, Catherine, Tizzie, Brigid, Maisie and Luna stood up and moved to stand behind Stella and Kai.

Logan and Angus and Blair shuffled up behind them. "Suppose we'd better help too."

"I'm glad you said that." Stella smiled. "Can you sit in on today's training, and after lunch take the armies out and set up in preparation for war against Mabel. We need to be in place, ready to fight, to distract Mabel, in case the banishment doesn't work."

His hand held beside his head in a salute, Logan indicated the empty platter in front of him. "I speak for the three of us when I say we're humbled to be able to assist. May we partake of some of the food and drink first? We've been days travelling and in need of sustenance."

Chapter Twenty Four

K^{ai} Three hours. That was all the time she had, to see her friends, possibly for the last time, if the excursion to the clock towers didn't go as planned. She met her friends in the school yard. The children, the orphans of the war that Cain created, were smiling as they chased each other around the yard. Three fairies hovered about, waving their wands, sending out clues that the children were tracking the magic to find the objects hidden in the magical garden beds that surrounded the courtyard.

"You've done an incredible job with these little ones." Kai said as she hugged her friends. Penne and Sage embraced her so tightly she had to gulp for air. Tears ran down her cheeks as she realised, she didn't know when she'd be able to visit again.

Sage handed Kai a plate full of exquisite shortbreads, shaped like stars. "Fae cooking. The children love it." Kai sampled one of the pastries, her tongue tingling at the tantalising taste of sugary sweetness that was out of place in medieval Scotland.

"What's wrong?" Penne asked, her brow furrowed.

As she let the melt in the mouth biscuits pop and fizz in her mouth, she considered her response. "I'm happy to see you." Kai spoke the truth. She couldn't tell them her next adventure would take her away from them, possibly forever, depending on what happened in the next twenty-four hours.

As if reading her mind, Sage asked. "How long can you stay this time?" She wiped away a couple of stray wisps of her blonde hair from in front of her face.

"Not long, I'm afraid. Soon though, if all goes well, I'll be back for good." She added seeing the looks of despair on her friends faces. She missed them as much as they missed her.

Not fighters, the sisters were nurturers, teachers, caring for those too weak or young to care for themselves. "By the equinox, or if not by the solstice. The next one, not the one nearly a whole season away." Sage said. Kai detected a hint of determination in the voice of the softer of the sisters. She wrapped her arms round them both.

"That's the plan. To be reunited with you both and continue our adventures together." Kai watched as a little girl no taller than her knees, waddled up and wrapped her stubby little arms around Penne's leg. Hot tears welled in Kai's eyes. Her friends were family to these bubs. While she longed to help care for the little ones, first she had work to do, to ensure their safety. Before that, there was time for one other thing, something long overdue.

"You two go and settle the little ones and I'll heat up some stew for you. It's been a long day and many more to come." She swung her arms around shooing them away to see to the children.

"We only have broth." Penne's soft-spoken voice threatened to break, we've been keeping what little food we have for the children." Kai sensed the despair in her voice, and she got angry. This senseless war was all her cousin's fault.

"It's lucky I have a few surprises then." She made her voice sound cheerful. She rummaged around in the folds of her robes and found the food she'd foraged on the way to the cottage. Some berries, edible flowers, and a couple of gourds and swedes that weren't too ruined.

Her friends' eyes grew wide as she laid her spoils on the wooden table that ran the middle of the room. The little one peeping out from behind Penne's skirts, babbled something that Kai didn't understand. Penne picked the tot up and held her over the table where she picked up a bumpy old gourd and tried to shove it in her mouth.

"Not yet little one. Let me cook it for your mamas and tomorrow you can have some too." Kai gently prised the vegetable from her grasp. "Let me do this for you." She said sternly to her friends. "I learnt more than a little about cooking watching your mum and your aunt for all those years."

CAIN SHOOK HIS HEAD, as he peered through the window. How innocent and naive was his cousin. She disappointed him, running home to those two poor excuses for a coven. She could've been standing beside him as he won the war, instead of being just another captive. He gagged. How pathetic. Kai goo-ed and gaa-ed at the bairns and hugged her friends while he and the others in the coven were waging the battle of their lives. At least she'd given up on the idea of working against him. He wondered if she'd a nasty bump on the head. "I'll spare your life, dear cousin. You're neither threat nor ally." He sneered. A shame really, he'd grown to think that at last she'd returned to the fold, willing to fight beside him.

A huge head appeared in the window, blocking his view of his cousin. That dratted dragon again! Cain swiped at the big googly eyes in front of him. The image gave way, he stumbled and fell. A stabbing pain seared through his forehead, right between his eyes. A jabbing pain through his stomach. Where had he landed this time? He struggled to stand, but his feet slipped, unable to get a hold on the ground.

Mabel opened the door to the master's room, and found him sprawled out, flat on his stomach on the floor, passed out. She'd been planning to slowly poison their fearless leader; with the belladonna purchased from the travellers. At this point in time, it appeared she didn't need to. She'd keep an eye on him. As she quietly closed his door, locking it from the outside, she smiled to herself. It might be easier to take control than she'd first thought.

Chapter Twenty Five

S tella
        The complete darkness when she opened her eyes threw her. Where was the candle that should be sitting beside her mattress? Something wasn't right. The air felt different, a familiar energy she couldn't quite identify. The silence confused Stella. Why couldn't she hear any movement in the castle or the courtyard? There were always people moving about, whispering quietly to each other. Where were the smells? Animals, animal dung, food preparation, or campfires, always an aroma that caused Stella to wrinkle her nose. She sniffed the air with a frown.

Her fingers searched for her coat that she always lay over her feet as she slept, ready to grab it should she need to go somewhere in a hurry. Instead of the comforting woollen coat or the thick, rough wool of the blanket that normally lay over her, the material was cool, synthetic, like her quilt cover at home in Australia. She swung her legs out to climb up off the mattress and fell on her knees on the floor. A carpeted floor, not the wooden floor under her mattress.

"What the?" She felt around in the dark, her hand recognising the familiar square box of a bedside table, and the cold metal of the reading light. The room lit up as she touched the switch. She squeezed her eyes shut, slowly opening them, blinking against the harsh instant light. In the other realm light was gentler, subtle.

As her eyes finally adjusted to the light, she looked around the room. Her bedroom, in the cute cottage home she'd inherited from her friend, about a year ago. Her neighbour, Sheila, was looking after it and her kitten, while she was away. Sheila's relatives were always popping in to visit, and Stella offered the use of her cottage as extra accommodation, while she travelled overseas to study.

Travelling overseas wasn't entirely untrue, and easier to explain than *I'm away visiting another realm.*

"It's lucky no one is staying here at the moment." Stella muttered aloud. "Or I'd have ended up in bed with them." She shook her head, to clear the jet lag, crossing realms caused the same effect as travelling across time zones, as she'd discovered last year.

She retrieved her coat from the floor where it had fallen sometime during the night, shrugging it on out of habit, she wasn't cold, but the coat always came in handy. Her fingers curled around a crumpled piece of paper in the pocket. She un-crumpled the ball of paper, hoping to find a note or a clue of some kind. No words were scribbled on either side.

"Maybe it'll make sense after coffee." She muttered. Turning a light on in every room, she checked cupboards and behind doors. No sinister monsters or witches waiting to jump out and harm her. Each corner of her pretty home the same as when she left it. A sigh of relief escaped her lips, unaware she'd been holding her breath. Stella inherited most of the furniture with her home. All too pretty to move on, her librarian friend's décor matched hers exactly. She smiled, the quaint wooden pieces reminding her of her friend. Now she was home, could she stay? Did she have to go back to the other realm? A week before Christmas last year, she'd waved her daughters off on their European adventures, handed her keys to Sheila and moved to medieval Dumfries. Now it was March. So much had happened in such a short time. It felt surreal being back, when only a few hours ago she'd been planning a spell to banish all evil, from the safety of a fairy's castle centuries away.

The digital clock on the oven revealed it was nearly five in the morning, the eerie glow out the window confirmed daylight wasn't far away. Should she be worried about her friends? Were they all safe, or caught up in some evil trap? This time it wasn't like the last time she'd found herself back in her time. Last time, kidnapped by travellers working for Cain, she'd found herself in Brisbane, an area she didn't know and with memory loss. Her brain wasn't foggy or heavy, but she couldn't remember why she'd returned home.

"I don't think I've been drugged or had a spell cast on me. I feel normal. I've come here to find a clue. The answer is on this piece of paper." She held the paper up as the kettle whistled away on the bench. The daddy long legs dangling on the venetian blinds plopped himself down next to the coffee tin Stella found in the pantry cupboard.

She inhaled the aroma of the coffee, as she scooped a generous amount into her mug. Having appreciated that Brigid magicked her coffee in medieval Scotland, it wasn't the same as instant made early in the morning, from a kettle and stirred with intent. The date on the long-life milk in the fridge informed her it should be good to use. A quick sniff confirmed it wasn't sour. Stella trickled a little into the mug as she stirred, thinking about what she needed to know. "Why I ended up here and how to get back, for a start."

The spider moved, and she watched fascinated, as he used four of his eight legs to manoeuvre the scrap of paper over to the kettle. He then nimbly climbed up the venetians until he was level with the spout of the kettle.

"No way!" Stella gasped as she held the piece of paper up to where the steam was lazily floating up and out of the hole in the kettle. Words formed on the once blank note.

Munro and Kellie. Clock Tower. 0600

The spider waved. Stella waved back. "Thanks."

She shoved her hands back into the pockets of her coat hoping for another clue. Her fingers found a mobile phone. Her mobile phone, fully charged according to the blinking battery light in the top corner of the screen. The screen confirmed the time - a little after five in the morning. The warmth of the coffee wove its magic, the kick of energy propelling her into action. She rinsed the cup and left it in the sink, the coffee tin away in the cupboard, the milk in the fridge. The apple and the chocolate bar, the items in the otherwise empty fridge seemed to be there for her, she took them, munching on the apple as she turned off all the lights in the house. She closed the front door behind her, quietly, and walked along the footpath towards the town.

Her mobile confirmed the location of the clock tower - on the corner of Munro and Kellie Streets, about two kilometres walk from her house. Scanning the information on her phone, the history behind the ruin, riddled with rumours of magic curses, covens meeting and black magic. "Makes as much sense as anything." She muttered, pulling her coat tightly around her as the early morning chill snuck under her coat, seeping through her jeans into her pores. The temperature in medieval Scotland was often freezing, but this early morning Aussie autumn was colder. A different cold, that crept into her bones.

It struck her as strange that she had woken in clothes from her time and not those she wore in the other realm. Jeans, a shirt and jumper. Clothes from her wardrobe here, though she had no memory of changing clothes, or arriving back in her cottage. At least she wasn't wandering around in robes from medieval Scotland. No need to attract too much attention. Her heart beat a little faster. What was she walking into? What would she find at the clock tower? Why her memory was hazy around this part of the plan, she wasn't sure. Intuition told her that she would remember when she needed to.

An early morning jogger brushed past her on the path, bringing her focus back to the present. Before she could apologise for getting in the way, another two joggers pushed past, causing her to walk on the wet grass.

Move.

That little voice, her intuition whispered urgently. Stella stepped off the concrete path and headed for the road. Void of cars, so she quickly crossed to the other side. Using the telephone box to shield her, she watched the road. Three groups of joggers, all in the black like the first two, passed by. The number of the original members of the Mark of the Thirteen Coven. A coincidence? All heading away from the clock tower. Considering the area was popular with local fitness fanatics, maybe she was overthinking it.

Quickening her pace Stella turned the corner and ran into the back of someone.

"Excuse me, I'm sorry."

The person in front of her turned around. "Stella!" Kai hugged her. "I'm so pleased to see you. Do you know why we're here?"

Her energy calmed significantly, finding her friend in the middle of the path to the tower. "I think it has something to do with banishing Cain and his coven."

Three colourful lights flew into view. As they got closer, three fairies from Broomhilda's family came into view. Dressed in tiny dresses that matched their hair, lime, pink, and baby blue. Their wings shone in the morning light. Without a word, the pink fairy motioned for Stella and Kai to follow them. The lights stopped in front of a tall concrete structure that Stella remembered passing by many times, without really noticing it. A depressing grey, with graffiti trawled all over it, the energy it gave off - of desolation, frustration and anger.

"Before you get any closer to the clock tower, we need to tell you why you're here." The fairy with green hair whispered lyrically. "Yesterday you prepared to banish the coven, with a plan that included clock towers and fae enchantments. Brigid, Tizzie, Catherine, Luna, Maisie, Broomhilda, Logan, Angus, and Blair are at other locations, receiving the same advice. You cast a protection around those who were travelling to the clock towers, so you could move freely without malevolence following you. Do you remember?"

As soon as the fairy began to speak, the blanket of protection vanished, Stella remembered the plan. "Yes! We're using the clock towers negative energy to banish the evil." Kai nodded. Both woman's memories returned. The dark energy of the clock tower vibrated, trying to grab their energy. "Careful!" Stella shoved the energy back with her hands, as a thread of white energy caught the grey cloud that was floating around them. The thread wrapped itself around the grey, tethering it back onto itself. The light and grey throbbed together. A weird humming noise came from the mass.

"You have to hurry." The blue fairy whispered. "You need to strike before Cain does."

Kai turned grey; her face looked worse than the pulsing cloud hanging from the side of the tower. "What's wrong?" Stella watched the colour drain from Kai's face.

"I think I'll need to get to Cain, for the banishment to work, I have to be with him." Kai stated, dread filling her from deep in her toes.

Chapter Twenty Six

L una

The last time Luna tried scrying to locate her children, a swirling dense fog escaped the crystal ball, chilled the air around, and her threatened to consume her. Many years ago, when her children were very young.

She knew they were alive now, older, maybe even looking for her, though Kai said they likely didn't remember who they were, or used to be. Her hands trembled as she pulled her quartz ball from the bottom shelf. Her fingers stuck together as she lifted the black velvet cloth off the crystal. The glow from the object hurt her eyes. Luna knew she could have asked Catherine and Tizzie to be there with her, but she didn't want to get her hopes up, or anyone else's. Her friends still blamed themselves for her children's disappearance. If she hadn't stayed to help rid the realm of evil, they may never have been ripped away from her.

If she found her children, the crone would tell everyone, and celebrate for days, if the ball didn't reveal their whereabouts, then no one else need to feel bad for her. The palms of her hands, and her fingers tingled as she moved them closer to the crystal ball. She focused on the feeling of her children, as adults, rather than the children they once were. The images quickly formed in her mind. Slowly she opened her eyes

She blinked her eyes tightly shut then opened them again.

Not sure what she expected to see, the image in front of her was not what she expected.

Not yet. Soon.

The words in written form, felt icky. Luna dropped her hands away from the ball. Never in any of her years scrying had the result yielded words, rather than images. She'd hoped at least to confirm whether they were living in this realm or back in the land where they were born. Were the words from her children, someone who was helping, or one of malevolents?

The next words left no doubt in the crone's mind where the words came from.

Help me win and be reunited with your children.

Luna spun around, half expecting to see Cain standing behind her. Did he have hidden cameras in the castle? Unlikely but she knew not to underestimate the fiend who stole her children. She reigned in her anger, though she felt like throwing the crystal ball across the room. Instead, she covered the ball with its velvet cloth, and as she returned it to its hiding place, she muttered, "Damn thing's broken. Oh well, kids gone, what's next? I know! I'll make a potion to find my kitten, he's around here somewhere." She lifted her skirts and peered under the shelves, hoping that any evil doers would think her loopy and leave her alone.

The whoosh of air that lifted her books, crashing them down into a cloud of dust on her workbench didn't phase her. "Crazy critter, I know your hiding somewhere." Luna picked up each book, looking under as if she expected to see a kitten chasing the dust bunnies. The door to the apothecary swung open, banging shut as Cain, or whichever of his henchmen watching her, gave up and left. Still, Luna plonked herself down on the ground, one of her books open in front of her for a few minutes to be sure they'd gone.

Surer than ever that her children were alive. The crone smiled. Hopefully Cain witnessed her display of craziness, convincing him that Luna was alone and that the others were scattered.

"THE OLD CRONE IS OFF with the fairies." Cain scoffed to Mabel. "She won't be of any use, but she's no danger to us. Without her, her coven won't be bothered fighting a war they can't win. So much for the bravest and strongest fairy in the world leading an army against us." The coven leader chuckled at his superiority. "Her team seems to be falling apart."

Mabel stared at the master, once fearless and focused, babbling like a mad man, as loopy as the crone he was muttering about. She nodded, encouraging him to keep talking.

"I'm almost tempted to offer Kai a place by my side again. I'm not convinced she isn't working to undermine the goodie two shoes, before claiming her rightful place with us." His ego grew at the thought. In his deluded mind, he towered over Mabel, though she was only a few centimetres shorter, and wiry. He sneered down at her, totally unprepared for what happened next.

The kick caught him on his shins, Mabel's boot flew into his leg, he tumbled and fell on his knees. Mabel jumped to one side to miss being crushed by his frame. As he struggled to his feet, Mabel held out her hand to help him up. "You must be exhausted master. Why don't you rest? I've got a nice drink of mead for you, to help you sleep. I'll call for you if there's any news."

Cain snatched the tankard and skulled the contents, which included belladonna that Mabel added to every meal he took. "If I didn't know better, I'd have said you kicked me. It was one of those blasted dragons. We must get rid of the dragons. Get onto it Mabel. While I rest, you'll rid our castle of those fiendish fire breathing creatures once and for all." He waved his arm in the air, dismissing his second in charge.

Mabel clenched her fists. With every fibre of her body, she wanted to ram her knife so far into the master's chest that it came out the other side. Instead, she threw her knife at the pile of books on his bench. "Damn dragons." She said, turning and throwing her second knife so it flew inches from her leader's head. It was difficult not to laugh at the look on his face.

Cain shook his head, voices whispering, a buzzing he couldn't shake. "There's a room I want to show you, where we can lock the dragons to keep them away from us."

Mabel eyed her leader. She shrugged. It'd do no harm to humour him, he was no threat to her anymore.

"Let me show you the strength of the vault." Cain steered Mabel out of his quarters, along the corridor to the hidden room that he'd enchanted so that no one else would find it.

Mabel followed his lead and placed her hands behind her back, though her fingers were itching for the cool steel blade.

The coven leader stepped up to the metal door hidden in the grey stone wall at the end of the corridor. He held his hand out, twisting the large metal key embedded in the ancient lock. The door swung open inwards. He led her through into the vault. This prison he'd hoped never to have to use, but he distrusted that look in his army chief's eyes. She was hungry for blood, ruthless, and becoming unhinged. An asset as a warrior and leader of his army, such a shame her blood lust made her a liability now. The days ahead required concentration, considered, measured and careful manipulation, not masses of bloodshed, now that Broomhilda and her army were in tatters.

"What's this?" Mabel indicated a large metal sword attached to a chain in the middle of the room.

"Go ahead. See how it feels." He knew she wouldn't be able to resist. He stepped back away from her as she reached out to caress the metal blade. As soon as her long fingers touched that steel, the chains wrapped around her. She opened her mouth, but no sound came out. The more she struggled and tried to scream, her panic rising, the tighter the chains became.

His face contorted into what he thought was a smile. Others would have considered it a sneer or a grimace of pain. "Such a shame. You were a good warrior."

Mabel's face, crushed by the chain, the pain wracking her body.

Cain turned and left; the door closed behind him and faded back into the stone wall.

Chapter Twenty Seven

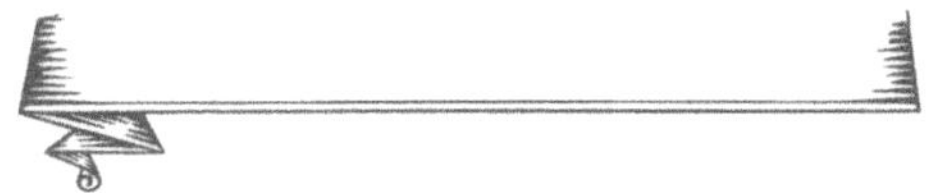

Broomhilda

So peaceful for the oldest fairy - twenty-four hours since Broomhilda had seen another living being. The fairy glen was full of flora and fauna, birds, insects and tiny animals, all of whom were content to let the tiny being rest under the branches of the ancient tree. Could it be too quiet?

Her yearning for years of peace and quiet, away from the drama, the busy-ness of life was waning. Whilst she initially craved the peace, under the shade of her old friend, her fingers tapped on the ancient bark, her toes wriggled in the cooling stream. No one asking her for advice. No fairies to teach, no plans to make, no gardens to tend or schools to oversee. Calm, quiet, save for the chatter of the animals, the twitter of the birds and the shrilling of insects. Absolutely nothing she needed to do.

"I'm so bored." She told Gertrude, who'd come looking for her, to fill her in on the goings on at the castle.

"So does that mean you're coming home?" Gertrude didn't like the fairy glen as much as her older sibling. The younger sister thrived on the energy of others, the sounds, the tastes, smells and sights, all the things that exhausted Broomhilda.

The elder sister sighed. "I don't need to. It sounds like Stella has everything under control."

"Are you sure?" Gertrude persisted. "There's something about the spell they're going to invoke. A memory from times long past or something I read once. We're missing a piece of information."

The older sibling gazed up through the canopy, to the very top of the oldest tree. Speckled sunlight trickled through, shining brightly, as were the specs of the blue sky dotted between the leaves. Flashes of colour splashed between the lush green, as birds darted between branches, singing to each other. She glimpsed, out of the corner of her eyes, little woodland creatures, scurrying on the forest floor of sticks, twigs and fallen leaves. She sighed again. If only she wasn't bored. Then she could stay here forever and not get drawn back into the drama.

"You didn't choose this life. It chose you. You're the first born. Destined to help protect the world from evil." Gertrude touched her sister, lightly. These sisters didn't normally do touchy feely. "It's natural to feel exhausted, worn out, and crave the quiet, it's been a constant battle. But I know you sister, and if there's any chance that evil will win and seep into the fairy realm, you'll fight, even when you've nothing left to give."

Raising one eyebrow, trying to look stern, Broomhilda raised herself to stand at her full height, a smidgeon taller than her sister. *By a mouse's whisker,* one of her elderly relatives used to say when the younger one complained. She moved over to the ember of the magic fire she'd lit earlier, scrying, because of the boredom, and the need to be useful, to know that everything was alright. She waved her hand over the remains of the fire, sprinkling some dust she found in her pocket.

Orange and yellow sparks flew up from the fire. The crackling sound no louder than a cicada calling to its mate somewhere in amongst the under growth. The flames rose as tall as the shortest blade of grass, no taller than the fairy's kneecaps and absolutely no danger to the landscape at all. Gertrude copied her sister, sprinkling some dust from her pocket. The flames and the smoke changed colour to shades of blue and green. The wisdom of the elements – fire, earth, air and water joined with spirit as the sisters gazed into the magic fire.

As they gazed, images ran like a movie reel, through the embers. "Our ancestors fought evil, thousands of years ago, hundreds of years ago. What we're facing is nothing new." Gertrude mused. "I've heard of most of these tales. It's eerie watching them play out in front of us. There's a pattern here, a message. I think we're meant to find it."

Broomhilda agreed. "Maybe we can ask those who have fought the evil before, what we need to know." She wasn't hopeful; she wracked her brain to try and remember. "It's as if I know the answer, it's just out of reach." Her eyes wandered to the array of bright coloured flowers dotted along the edge of the stream. "Snap dragons. Breaking curses."

"It that important?" Her sister asked.

"Dragons, snap dragons, breaking curses or stopping curses being cast. I'm not sure what I'm meant to know or remember." And yet something about the flowers...

SNAP DRAGONS, PLANTED in the garden during its construction, protected the castle, and Cain from anyone who tried to harm him. The vison that kept haunting him, of Mabel poisoning him, had come to pass. "I've seen the future." He boosted to those gathered in the dining hall. "Mabel set out to kill me, to drive me mad. I've taken care of her, and I'll take care of anyone else who seeks to harm me, or any of my coven."

His ego, he wouldn't for one moment entertain the idea that any of his coven would welcome Mabel as leader. Quietly, to themselves, most of those who were listening to him, wished Mabel had been successful. Each wondered if there was a way to destroy the protection, so that he could be usurped. Not that anyone present in the room thought themselves leadership material.

"As much food and drink as you want. Eat, drink and be merry. We will be victorious!" Cain left the dining hall. Off in search of dragons. The castle protection didn't afford the master a shield against insanity.

THE FAE SISTERS FLEW to the edge of the realm. The place where the edges blurred, a veil of mystical fog permanently shielded the magic folk, offering sanctuary to pure hearted beings. An enchantment from so long ago no one, not even these two fairies, knew how to change it. "This is good. The border's still active." From their position in the canopy of branches, the place where the other realms butted up against each other barely visible, a myriad of shimmering colours, home to a variety of magical creatures.

"I don't know what we're looking for." Gertrude said.

"Neither do I, everything looks as I expected. No ominous dark clouds or bubbles of malevolent energy. Maybe we will be okay after all." Her hand lightly touched her younger sister's arm, a tingling energy, unique to fairies, shot through both fairies' bodies. "I think we'd better go back, but first there's an enchantment to invoke. An ancient, added layer of safety over the realms."

The sisters flew around together, darting in and out of the sentry trees and the mist that swirled around the edge of the realm. Their voices joined as they chanted. "*By the power of the air we breathe, the water that gives us life, the fire that purifies, and the earth beneath our feet. Spirit goddess, mother earth, we ask for clarity, for protection, for focus and success in our endeavours. For purity, minds that are clear for the quest, hidden from the evil. For the success of the enchantment to banish the evil from all realms.*"

They repeated the chant, three times, ending with the words, "So mote it be."

Chapter Twenty Eight

K^{ai} Kai turned slowly, taking in the details of the concrete block that loomed menacingly over them, the clock tower blocked the sun as it climbed rapidly above the horizon. "Something doesn't feel right, we don't both need to be here." She glanced around at the worn brick homes, where families were waking up, starting their day; the kettle boiling, tea bags dipped into cups, bread in the toaster waiting for butter and jam. Out of their chimneys smoke spewed, merging with the lower cloud layer that hung ominously lower than normal. The heaters, stoves and fireplaces warming the toes of those frantically looking for lost socks, thick jumpers and snacks for school.

"It feels a little odd." Stella admitted, the skin on her arms tingled, the hairs on her arms prickled under her top she was wearing as she looked around. "Something is out of place, out of time."

Kai knew what she had to do. Stella knew it too.

Hecate's voice that confirmed it. "Beguile him, distract him. If your intent is pure, as I know it is, you won't be banished, you'll find your way back here." Stella embraced Kai, who pulled away first, fearful she'd stay if she didn't. Neither wanted Kai to leave, both knew she must.

"I'll see you soon." Kai hoped her words were true, as she headed back to the castle of her nightmares. The portal Stella had opened closed so quickly after her, she nearly tripped on it. She slowed her breathing as she found herself walking briskly along the corridor to her cousin's quarters.

"WE NEVER DISCUSSED my reward, but I think a share in the power and magic is fair reward for tearing apart our opposition." She walked straight in without knocking, knowing she had to match his bravado to be convincing. Finding the strength to speak with as much authority as she could, the way he always spoke to her.

"There you are. I wondered if you'd return or if you'd gone to the dark side." Her cousin as full of ego as ever. The darkness of his aura emanated more strongly than she remembered it before, surprised the potion they given them had worn off so quickly. She'd made the right decision, as long as she could pull this off. He needed to believe her performance.

"I'm on the side of family, our family. It was almost too easy to scatter those do-gooders." Kai considered her words. "They were so trusting, they let me get into their heads. They believed me, all the lies I spun about me being on their side. It helped that I was able to slip a concoction of herbs into their food. The crankiness the potion caused made them fight amongst themselves. Luna became loopier than usual, her grasp on reality is almost non-existent."

"Why should I believe you?" Cain eyed his cousin suspiciously. At least the dragons were absent for now. He must have scared them away. "All reports told me you were getting chummy with Stella." He spat that witches name out, as if it were a mouthful of hot chilli. "Then you disappeared. Did you go back to the modern world, or to your coven?"

Kai knew better than to think this an innocent question. He was testing her. Luckily, she'd rehearsed answers to the most likely questions. She noted the piles of books on the floor, several empty plates and cups strewn around the room. Her cousin's room was normally pristine. He hated mess. Maybe he suffered the effects of their potions after all.

"I visited both the modern world and Penne and Sage." Kai confirmed. "I needed to retrieve a package I'd hidden there when I was spying on Stella. Some of the herbs are easier to source, as modern medicine than they are here." That was true at least, that modern medicine did contain some of the more poisonous herbs. The skill came in understanding the correct dosage and knowing how to use them effectively. "I checked in on Penne and Sage, because whether you approve or not, they're friends." She chose the word friend specifically knowing if she called them family that it could irritate Cain. "You'll keep your promise not to harm them." She spoke firmly, showing no weakness.

Cain considered his response. With Mabel indisposed he could use another gullible person to do his bidding. To act as intermediary between himself and the others. It would free him up to contemplate all that he'd do once he'd stolen the power and the magic for himself. She could start by cleaning up the mess in the room. He sniffed, the pungent aroma of the food rotting on the plates may be attracting the dragons.

Kai noticed Cain's twitch. Was he hallucinating? She crossed her arms in front of her chest and waited.

"You can start by cleaning up this mess. Bring me more mead and some food. I'm hungry." He swept his arm to encompass the chaos in front of them. "After that I need you to lead the army for the attack. You know where the castle is. That won't be a problem, will it?" He shoved his face so close to Kai's it took all her will power not to gag.

"It's not a problem for me. As you pointed out, I can lead the army right to the castle. Won't Mabel want to take the lead? She's trained our army for months."

"Mabel is no longer a part of our coven. She chose to leave." Cain wasn't about to share the location of the secret vault with his little cousin. Unless one day she earnt the right for it to become her final resting place.

That piece of information was unexpected. Mabel wouldn't have voluntarily left the coven. The more likely scenario, that Cain discovered Mabel's plan, and she became a threat to his leadership. Kai made a note to see if any of the other coven members knew where Mabel had gone.

"In that case, I'd be honoured to lead our army." She replied to her cousin, allowing her mouth to show a hint of a smile.

Cain nodded curtly and turned away, signalling the end of the conversation.

Kai, thankful for no more small talk, piled the plates together, and balanced the tankards on top. She trod carefully so as not to drop them, as she headed to the kitchen.

Madge, the cook from her childhood, and the other servants, she'd met the last time she stayed at the castle, were in the kitchen. Madge and the youngsters enveloped Kai in a hug that lasted longer than it should if she were to convince the master of her loyalty. Cain knew she'd spent hours in the kitchen with Penne, Sage and their aunt Madge, after her parent died. Maybe he'd think twice before trying to step in the way of her friendship with the staff. "We're so glad you're back." Scarlett, the young servant girl she'd met last time, whispered into her neck as they hugged. The other woman in the kitchen, Kai vaguely recognised. Similar in age, or a couple of years older than herself, with blonde hair peppered with grey, the woman was taller than Kai.

"It's Kai isn't it?" The woman looked up from the swedes she was cutting and tossing into the large cast iron pot that hung low above the open fire. "We met years ago, at school, before we were sent home. We shared a couple of classes together. My name's Sophie."

"Of course, I remember. We were in Math and Potions together. What made you decide to work here?"

"My mum got sick. She couldn't take in mending anymore. I sew by night and cook during the day. It pays good money; Madge got permission from the master, there's too much work now, for one cook, with many people living in the castle." Sophie dropped the last of the vegetables into the pot. Water splashed and bubbled as the gourds made their place in the stew.

"Speaking of the master, he's asked for some food and something to drink. Do you mind if I put a tray together for him?"

Sophie nodded, pointing to the trays piled high with meats and cheeses, waiting to be taken out to the dining hall. "Help yourself. He rarely eats with the others these days, since Mabel left."

Kai picked up an empty platter and piled some food on it for Cain. "I can take those trays to the hall for you, when I come back." She added casually. "Where did Mabel go?"

Sophie's voice was hushed. "All I know is that she left late one night. On foot. It's all very strange, as there'd been talk, she'd planned to challenge the master for the leadership." Putting her fingers to her lips as voices could be heard outside the kitchen. Kai nodded, knowing how dangerous it could be, to talk freely anywhere in this monstrosity of a castle, and left with the tray for Cain. Tempted to add a little something to the food, she decided not to, lest he taste it and think she was trying to poison him.

The master sat crossed legged on the floor. Books open around him; but staring at something in the corner. Something she couldn't see, but it clearly irritated him. He swiped his hand in front of him, shooing it away. As she lay the tray on the floor he nodded curtly, pretending something in the book was intriguing.

"I'll eat with the troops, get the army ready to attack first thing tomorrow." She said, quickly walking away, not liking the look of the crazed glint to his eye.

With platters of food already positioned on the table benches, Kai didn't have to help after all. A young lad with blonde hair followed Sophie, placing tankards of mead near the platters of food. Many of the coven members congregated around the tables. Sophie averted her eyes, the teen hurried behind her. Kai expected to see more people. If Mabel didn't have a team out training, or preparing for an attack, where were those who swore their loyalty to the master and his quest? If she wanted to learn the answers, she'd have to convince them she was back for good.

"Kai, you've returned." An arrogant male, with black wavy hair, around her age sneered. "We had bets on whether you were a traitor or whether you'd come back, tail between your legs, begging the master not to kill you. It appears I've lost the wager." He laughed, but there was no humour in it.

"If you find that funny, you're going to love this." Kai matched his arrogance. "The master's asked me to take Mabel's place and lead the army at first light tomorrow." She waited, for her words to sink in, around the table. Furious whispering, that she ignored, or at least pretended to, as she ate some bread that sat heavy in her stomach. Hopeful that hidden in the discussion and inevitable questions would be some useful answers. *Play it cool.* She didn't have to wait long.

"We don't mention that name here. When she left, she took half the coven with her." An older woman, with her grey hair tied up in a bun, called from the next table. "Full of bravado, that she was going to rule. Then suddenly, without a word, she skulked off in the dead of night. Her followers left the next day. A good thing too, if they hadn't the master would've exiled them."

Dinner with the coven. Even with reduced numbers, it made her skin crawl. Any hopes of finding members aligned with Mabel, faded fast. Those who remained were staunch supporters of Cain and his plans. In her gruffest voice, forcing the words out, in an attempt to gain kudos with the group, she barked. "At least those of us left behind are loyal. Tomorrow morning, be ready as soon as it's light. We've a full day's travel." She stood up. Calling on her strength to appear aloof and unapproachable as Cain was.

It worked. After a murmur of consent, they continued to fill their face, unperturbed by the change. Brainwashed by her cousin no doubt.

She felt a pulsing in her temple. Just as the fairy with the blue hair indicated, when the time was right, a vibration would emanate between the clock towers. They were ready! Not a moment too soon. The energy in the castle so dark, it was slowly sapping her strength. Cain grew crazier and more unstable, his power and energy throbbing through the castle walls. She'd underestimated how difficult this would be. The sweat beads on her brow tasted salty when she wiped her forehead, a few drops falling on her lips. Should she be facing him when they cast their spell, or was being close by enough?

"You're looking a little pale." A weaselly youth a little younger than Kai sidled up to where she'd plonked herself on one of the benches at the far end of the dining hall. She clenched her fists as a wave of vertigo hit her. Kai concentrated on her annoying neighbour, his hands grabbing two of everything on the platters in front of him. He wasn't portly, so much as slimy, she wondered how he'd eat that much without being the size of a bear. She reached for some bread and cheese, placing the cheese in front of her as she nibbled on the bread. "I'll be fine after I eat." The droning sound, was it in her head, or did the others hear it too?

Chapter Twenty Nine

S tella

Hecate afforded Stella a strength and more confidence than she normally possessed. Not a soul came out of any the houses in the street, no cars whizzed past, as she walked slowly up to the base of the concrete tower. It was as if time stood still. No dogs barked, no cats hurried home, the birdsong paused, as if the creatures were holding their breath. Even the sun appeared to stop moving, hovering not far above the horizon. Stella walked through to the hollow middle of the tower. Ghosts of previous enchantments whispered chants she heard and understood through Hecate's memories. It simultaneously made perfect sense and no sense at all.

The graffiti in this room reminded Stella of the sigils in the back of her Book of Spells. Hecate knew their meanings and which one to activate. The sigils pulsed and vibrated, reminding Stella of the ebb and flow of a river or an air current, or the flickering of flames, until one was so much stronger than the others. The wriggly line with the arrow facing north faded, as did the sun sign, the air, earth and water. The sigil glowed strong, the eye with the star over it beckoned. Stella stood so her left hand was on the fire, her other hand lay over the eye with the star. The jolt of energy shocked through her body, gritting her teeth she resisted the urge to pull her hand away. Words from long ago, forged within her memory, and the words the fairies left for her, lit up like holograms around the internal walls of the clock tower.

A cast iron cauldron, which should have looked out of place, hissed and popped as bubbles danced above it, stood to one side. Stella couldn't see an external heat source, it wasn't sitting on embers, fire or a gas stove. The heat of the water warmed her skin as she held her hands over the bubbles. A cloth lay next to the cauldron, with items laid across it. A pouch of herbs, a small amber bottle of liquid, three dark stones, a shell and a black feather.

The connection with her friends strong, she dropped each item into the cauldron. She watched the herbs trickle out of the pouch. As the liquid dripped from the bottle into the bubbles, a fizzing sound emanated from deep inside the pot. The stones clunked to the bottom, the shell and the feather took longer to sink. The chanting in her head, the words on the walls around her, louder and louder, echoing between the clock towers. Her body burned, an internal energy lit in all those with pure intent, to banish the evil once and for all. The bond, the connection between those she trusted, who were all bravely helping her defeat the coven and restore the balance. As she repeated the words a third time, the grounds and the walls around her shook.

Words flashed in front of her eyes, and images of wars long ago, brutal, swords and knives, bodies strewed in a field, blood turning the ground red. Limbs amputated, others lying face down in a lake. Stella shuddered as image of Kai, being knocked around by the enchantment, came into view. Her presence at the castle necessary for the success of the banishment. Kai knew the risk when she volunteered to confront her cousin. Stella's heart dropped to her stomach, realising that if Kai still linked in the slightest way with the malevolence, or entwined in the ways of the coven, she would be exiled forever, or worse.

Drawing herself up to her full height, Hecate reached her hands up, touching the stone in the chamber inside the structure. Under her breath she muttered the words of the ancient fae enchantment. Her words carried the power of her years, and her ancestors before her. Stella's voice joined with Hecates, and the other witches, at their various posts throughout the realms.

Opposites unite in the quest for purity, innocence, truth and freedom,
Release our realms from the evil who seeks to overcome us.
Remove them from our lands forever and a day.
Powers of the seasons, of the elements and our ancestors send the evil away.
(The last stanza of this poem fae words, spoken only for to write them down
would diminish their power)
By the power of Hecate, Broomhilda and the oldest and most powerful good in
this world
This enchantment will remain in place forever

So mote it be.

AT THEIR RESPECTIVE posts, the clock towers throughout the land, those aligned with good noticed the shift in the energy. Each team, their intuition and connection guiding them – to repeat the enchantment for the spell to purge all evil from the land. Chanting loudly, their surroundings shook, the air around them grew thick, their throats burned, their hands shook, their temples pulsed as the ancient energy coursed through their veins.

Luna swiped the air around her with her hands, swinging her arms wide. She gulped, the air thick making it difficult to breathe. *Stay focused. You can do this.* Whispered her spirit guides, those who kept her safe throughout her life. Her feet stamped the ground, gathering her energy, gathering her strength to continue, to see this through to the end. No time for distractions now.

STELLA DIDN'T KNOW what she expected, but as she finished the third chant, there was no thunder, or lightning, the sky didn't fall, and the magpies started warbling to each other in the gum trees a few houses away. She lowered her hands, the electricity tingling through her fingers as she shook them. Her legs wobbled, her feet trying to locate even ground, to steady herself against the power of the experience.

The ground, the tower, slowly stopped shaking. Her eyes focused as the thick foggy air in front of her evaporated. The words, the sigils and even the cauldron that had been bubbling away while she chanted the ancient words – all disappeared. The structure, the clock tower, lost its shimmer. Every last ounce of magic in it gone, it became an abandoned building again.

A movement on the other side of the road startled her; her body flinched as if she'd been struck. She took a deep breath in and out, to calm her senses, still on hyper alert after the incantation. The boy was probably twelve years old, with his backpack sitting heavily on his shoulders as he slammed his front door shut and loped down the footpath. A car drove past, beeping it's horn at the dog who was wandering along the side of the road. No danger. Ordinary life, jarring, as she came back to the present, to the ordinary.

Had they succeeded? Life seemed unchanged here, in this suburb of Australia's capital. Kids were off to school; people were off to work, and dogs were out on adventures. She thought there'd be some clue that they'd won the war, that somehow, she'd know. Of course it wasn't going to be that easy. She sighed, a horrible sinking feeling rising from her toes, an indication that it hadn't gone according to plan. Stella looked around the neighbourhood and headed back to her cottage.

When her mobile beeped, indicating a message, Stella fumbled in the pocket of her coat to find it. Fingers twitching as she swiped the screen. The message wasn't from any of the coven, which made sense, as this technology didn't exist in their realm.

The message from her children, that they were having a so much fun and had decided on a road trip to Scotland. Was there a reason why they were headed to Scotland? Cain? Another deep breath to calm her emotions, she wasn't going to win the war and lose her children. She re-read the message. *Off to Europe, then to Scotland*. It would've been rude to ask *Why?* Instead, she messaged back: *Wow! Awesome adventures! Have fun. Can't wait to hear more about your travels*. Patience, not one of her virtues, nor trust, she decided it was time to practice both, and to believe her children were safe and living their best lives.

Home felt like home. The garden she'd started, the kitten, the house, all hers, no one could take it away from her. She didn't want to leave, but she must return to her coven, to confirm their safety and the success of the spell.

Her neighbour, Sheila, with a bun of bright blue hair piled up high on her head, an old straw hat with the top cut out to accommodate the hair was watering her prize-winning roses, camellias, and gardenias. "There you are Stella, I thought I saw the lights on early this morning. My friend who I lined up to house sit for you, ended up taking a job in Perth so I'm looking after your cottage, and Puddles of course." Sheila spoke quickly, as if she hadn't spoken to anyone forever. Right on cue, a little bundle of fluff flew over and climbed up Stella's leg.

"Puddles! It's so good to see you. My you've grown, but still my little precious." Stella scooped the fluffy bundle into her arms, nuzzling her face against his fur. How easy it would be to stay here, snuggling her familiar and planning her trip to see her children.

"Are you back for good?" Stella wasn't sure how to answer her well-meaning, inquisitive neighbour's question. Sheila wasn't a busy body as much as curious and loved company. Always up for a cuppa and a chat. They'd many discussions about her prize winning garden and had been invaluable when Stella decided to plan a garden out the back, past the verandah and the clothesline. She did miss time out in her garden, fingers in the dirt, making mulch and nurturing the lavender, the rosemary, geraniums and anything else that grew in in the soil.

"I've got a job I must finish, then yes, I'll come back for a while. It might have to be six months and six months there. The works too good to pass up the opportunity." Stella couldn't remember what story she'd given her neighbour when she chose to move to the realm for a few months. She hoped she'd been deliberately vague and that embellishing it now would not cause any curiosity. "The program I developed here, for young children, is proving popular around the state. Down south and up north too." She ad libbed, hoping she'd remember her story next time she saw her neighbour.

After what seemed like ages, she finally managed to extricate herself from the friendly conversation, fibbing that she'd an online call scheduled she had to prepare for. She carried Puddles inside. She sat him on the floor as she filled the kettle. "While that heats up, I'm having a shower, a long, hot shower, with soap and shampoo." She whispered to her familiar.

"The things I take for granted." Stella told Puddles as she sipped her coffee ten minutes later. "Hot and cold running water, electricity, real instant coffee. And you. I missed you so much. I promise I'll be back as soon as I can." She scooped her kitten up, burying her face in his soft fur. She didn't have a familiar in the other realm. There were plenty of cats, that lived in the village and at the castle, but none were specifically hers. One last drink drained the cup, she rinsed it and returned it to the cupboard.

No longer able to ignore Hecates voice, the call to return to the realm and finish the task grew stronger each minute. Stella scribbled a note for Sheila and gave Puddles a big hug. Her heart torn into three, why couldn't Puddles, her kids and her coven all live in the same town, the same country, or the same world?

Hoping the portal in the back of the cupboard in the spare room would still take her to somewhere close to the castle, Stella pushed aside the old coat and shawl and slipped through the shimmering purple curtain.

The cobblestones cold under her knees as she stumbled, tripping over the corner of her coat. It took a couple of seconds for Stella to register the noise of the people gathered in the middle of the square, where the markets were normally held.

Who were they and why were they yelling?

Chapter Thirty

K^ai Kai's heart was thumping, loudly. Her blood pumping through her veins, lightheaded and dizzy, it took all her strength to ignore her physical symptoms. She forced one foot in front of the other determined to get as close as possible to her cousin, for the success of their mission. A movement down the corridor caught her eye. She leant against the nearest wall for support, her knees trembled as the ground beneath her feet shook. The malevolent leader was walking towards her, towards the dining hall. More accurately he was stumbling, tripping over his feet and his robes as he strode towards his coven.

Her protection shields firmly in place, she centred herself, connecting to the energy of Stella. No one in the dining hall seemed to notice anything unusual about Kai. With her head bowed a little so no one could see her muttering the enchantment, she moved to where she could keep an eye on her cousin and the dining hall.

Muttering the enchantment, the words fell out of her mouth easily, her voice grew stronger with each word, her words joining with those of the other members of the coven, her coven, born not of birth but of the desire to do the right thing. Kai's one thought, to defeat the coven, to banish them forever and free the world from evil, the words came easily, intuitively.

Opposites unite in the quest for purity, innocence, truth and freedom,
Release our realms from the evil who seeks to overcome us.
Remove them from our lands forever and a day.
Powers of the seasons, of the elements and our ancestors send the evil away.
(The last stanza of this poem fae words, spoken only for to write them down
would diminish their power)

By the power of Hecate, Broomhilda and the oldest and most powerful good in this world

This enchantment will remain in place forever

So mote it be.

The ground shook beneath the castle. Dust blurred her vision, as cracks appeared in the stone wall closest to her. Kai squinted, trying to find her cousin. Silhouettes of Cain and the others, faded in and out, like images in the static on an old black and white television. Their screams were muffled, as if from behind a door. An inhuman screech, unmistakably Cain's voice. Kai couldn't see what was happening, but it didn't sound pleasant. She kept the enchantment going.

What about Madge and the servants? A lump formed in her throat. What would happen to them? They weren't malevolent so surely; they wouldn't be harmed. She daren't leave her post before the enchantment completed. The third run of the spell now, her words grew louder, not caring if Cain realised she's aligned herself with Stella and Broomhilda. Kai edged closer to see what was happening with her own eyes.

Cain and the people standing closest to him faded, their images blurred around the edges like ghosts who haunted the castle. The look of absolute horror on Cain's face was clear, even with the dust and the commotion as the other coven members appeared to be suffering the same fate as their leader. Their mouths open, like their leader, their ear-splitting screams faded as part of the castle walls fell in the space between them. As she yelled the last few words of the enchantment, she pushed every ounce of her focus to banishing her cousin and his malevolent coven. The last word of the enchantment left her lips, as her legs gave way, crumpling beneath her, her energy expended.

A TUGGING ON HER ARM pulled Kai back to the present. She'd been trapped in a nightmare, being chased by Cain, who as a ghost was even angrier than in life. She flinched and lashed out her arm, in defence of whoever was trying to harm her.

"Ssh Miss Kai. It's Madge. Are you hurt?" the familiar voice of her dear friend, Penne and Sage's aunt penetrated the ghostly dream. Kai took Madge's her hands and eased herself up. Her feet and legs worked, nothing appeared to be broken. She flung her wobbly arms around her old friend, the person who'd been her rock, her maternal compass throughout her teen years.

"Madge! I'm so glad you're okay. What about the others? Scarlett, her siblings, and Sophie? Did they escape unharmed?" Kai blinked the dust from her eyes. She wiped the grit and dirt off her face. The haze, the rubble from the collapse of the castle, slowly settling into the land and the moat that used to skirt the fortress. Where it had once stood, tall, imposing, stones, remnants of wooden furniture, and metal that used to be the fortress, no longer dominated the landscape.

The dark sky above her full of stars, propelling an eerie light over the ruins of the castle and the paddocks beyond. Not too far from what would have been the entrance to the castle courtyard, Kai noticed a group gathered around a fire. With her arm around Madge, more for comfort then any need to be assisted in walking, she let her old friend lead her away from the mess that used to be the building where she lived. She shivered as she joined the others out in the field, the damp night air cutting through the layers of her clothing. Maybe jeans and a jumper, which helped her blend in, in Stella's world, wasn't such a great choice out here. Clothing in medieval Scotland made from thicker material than available in the modern world. The fire provided heat and added light in the cold dark night, Kai thawed, her bones, her skin, her heart, freed from the chains that tied her to The Coven.

The young blonde teenager, her hair plaited high up on her head in a bun that looked a little wonky, ran up and embraced Kai, knocking the breath from her lungs. "I'm so pleased you're safe. The others from the castle have vanished." Scarlett whispered excitedly. The young maid servant who'd she become friends with during her last visit to the castle, her cheeks rosy from sitting close to the fire, motioned for Kai to sit beside her. Her brother and sister crossed legged, not too close to the fire, smiled and waved at Kai.

Kai turned to Madge. "Is that true? Have the rest of the coven and their followers disappeared?" The butterflies in her stomach flip flopped. The last time she'd eaten anything, was an apple and a muffin, from the shop around the corner from Stella's house. The time difference confused her. "How long did I sleep?"

"Whoa, so many questions." Madge motioned for Kai to sit. "You were asleep for a small while. Angus, pass Kai some food." The young lad handed her a basket of sweetmeat and cheese.

"Now, you eat. You're still family to me, even if you're all grown up." Madge plonked herself down on Kai's other side warming her hands by the fire. "We were in the garden, making sure we'd enough vegetables for the evening meal. It was unusual, for us all to be out, but something told me we needed to be outside and away from the castle walls."

Scarlett nodded; eyes wide as she continued the story. "The ground shook, making our legs wobbly. We watched as the castle walls shook and crumpled and the whole building collapsed."

Feeling a little better, with a little cheese in her stomach, Kai asked. "How do you know that everyone else is gone? There might be bodies lying hidden in the rubble."

"I checked." Madge said gruffly. "There's no one else. We watched as a big portal of dark clouds hovered above the castle and sucked all the people up. I say people, they were more like ghouls, or demons." She shuddered. "Good riddance to them all."

"You were part of that coven, why didn't you get sucked up into the cloud?" Angus asked. Madge frowned at him and swiped her hand, though it didn't reach him.

"That's a good question." Kai swallowed the sweetmeat, adding to the lump of food lying in the pit of her stomach. "I was born into that coven, but I didn't belong to it. My coven is Penne and Sage, Madge's nieces."

Angus and his sister nodded. "Madge told us stories of how her nieces rescue lost children and look after them. They are very brave."

"Yes, they are brave. I met some other people, as brave as Penne and Sage, who disagreed with what Cain and his group stood for. We worked together to banish *The Mark of the Thirteen* from this realm once and for all. To be honest we didn't know if I'd get banished too. We hoped not. I knew I didn't belong with Cain." Kai fell silent, thankful she'd survived the enchantment, free to return to her friends.

"I'm so glad you're okay." Scarlet hugged Kai. "Can we meet the others who helped you?"

"I'm sure you can." Kai glanced at Madge. "Where are you planning on going now? If you come with me, I'll make sure you're safe. Would you like to work with Penne and Sage and help them look after the children at their school?"

Madge's face lit up at the mention of her nieces. "I'd like that very much. I could cook for them. Scarlett and the others could help with whatever they need." She said quietly. Scarlet clapped her hands together, her excitement bubbling over. Her brother and sister grinned as they hugged each other.

"Excellent! Now, does anyone know where there's a portal?" As Kai spoke, Angus pointed off to their right.

In the next field, a shimmering spec of light grew until it was the size of a door. "Is that a portal?" He asked.

Kai scrambled to her feet. "It sure is."

Chapter Thirty One

Luna

It was eerily quiet in the forest after Luna finished speaking the enchanted words aloud. The tree canopy and the clouds blocked what little warmth and light she expected to see from her vantage point near the old well. This part of the forest acted as a halfway point for travellers moving between realms. Trees hid portals and messages so that loved ones could safely communicate, and travel between realms to meet up and find each other. Bushes offered medicinal berries and fruits, none of them poisonous. The fae magic here too strong for any malevolence to exist. *The Mark of the Thirteen* couldn't transition through here. An urban myth Luna uncovered when she searched for her children, that The Coven sent the orphans they stole, to wait here, at this crossroads. What happened to the children next, no one knew.

A murmuring, she heard above the buzzing insects and the chirping birds, alerted Luna that others were entering the forest. She slid herself around to the back of the biggest tree she could find. From her vantage point she would see whoever entered the clearing before they saw her.

A crowd of people, too many to count, came into view. Luna's energy tingled with anticipation. The reason why became clear a few seconds later. She clasped her hand over her mouth to stop the gasp escape as she recognised one of the men. Freddie had been ten years old when she'd last seen him, but this was her first born, of that, she was sure. With his sandy hair, fair skin and green/blue eyes, he wasn't that different than the boy she lost. Taller of course. Her whole body longed to run to him and hug him for as long as the many years that he'd been lost. What had happened to him over the last twenty years and why was he here now, with so many others? Were these the lost children? Did the enchantment somehow free them from wherever they'd been since they'd been stolen? Where'd they come from? She chose to stay behind the tree and listen for clues.

"Did you see that?" The man to the left of Freddie asked. "As if they turned into ghosts and were sucked into the giant cloud?"

"I think it's called a vortex." Freddie responded. "Or a portal. Is it me, or do you feel lighter somehow? It's as if a weight's been lifted from my shoulders."

"I feel it too. Like all the evil in the world just vanished." Luna's heart was going to burst. That voice, the childlike innocence, it had to be Lizzie. The young lady had honey red hair, all tied up in a wispy ponytail high of top of her head. Could this be her third child? Were Annie and Katie somewhere in the crowd? She stood on tiptoes, stretching her neck to see if she could make out their faces in amongst the group of young people. Her intuition told her they were probably there, even though she couldn't see them.

A voice she didn't recognise spoke up from the other side of the group. One of the older women, judging by the tone of her voice. "I think we need to make a plan. In case they come back, or we find ourselves dragged somewhere else. A few minutes ago I was miles away from here, in a town south, setting up a market stall, though I saw the black cloud portal too. Next thing I know, here I'm in this part of the forest. I thought for a minute the master had found me and pulled me back to the castle."

A rumbling ran through the crowd.

"Does anyone actually know what happened?" A younger male voice asked. "Do we know who did this, whatever this is?"

Luna thought about responding. Her bottom lip quivered, her tongue felt odd. She opened her mouth to speak, but no words came out. She edged closer, lest they vanish before she got to see her children properly, but careful not to be seen. Dear goddess, she thought her heart was going to tear from her chest it was beating so rapidly.

"Something is different. I don't feel threatened or in danger. Like we don't have to do anything we don't want to." The young man with Freddie spoke again.

Before Luna was able to process those words, the older woman asked. "Could this be the day we've all been secretly hoping for?"

"I don't remember my life before The Coven. It's a blur. Every time I try to remember being a child, my parents, my family, I get a headache." Someone else called out.

A gentle breeze rippled through the forest. It caught a wisp of Luna's peppery grey hair, tucked up messily on the top of her head. Her hair tickled her neck. Goosebumps ran down the entire length of her arms. She leant forward in anticipation. She wished one of her children to speak again, so she could hear their voices.

"Me too." A flurry of voices echoed and at least half of those gathered raised their hands.

"It's as if we've been living in a fog, and now our memories are trying to return." Freddie mused. "I know I must've had a family, parents. I can feel them, here." Luna craned her neck and caught a glimpse of Freddie, as he took his hand from over his heart.

"Does anyone know where we are?" Lizzie's quiet voice, spoke from the middle of the crowd.

"I recognise the forest, and before you say all forests look the same this is the one I remember reading about. It's a safe place for people with good hearts to gather and get ready for the next part of their journey." A voice at the back of the group piped up. "I think I grew up in a market town, not far from here."

More people wandered into view, so focused on the conversation, she wasn't prepared, and realised her hiding place would be discovered. Luna edged a little further around the tree, desperate to hug her children, yet terrified of their reaction, if they didn't remember her. Did they remember each other? Had they been sent away together or separately? She clutched her stomach, the tightness there making her nauseous. She swallowed, and inhaled deeply, exhaling slowly, in an attempt to calm her body before it gave away her location. Prayed to the goddess for a happy ending.

"That's as good a place as any to start." Agreed the older woman. "Do you remember how to get there?"

Luna couldn't see if the woman nodded or not.

"Before we go any further can we place a protection spell over the group to keep us safe and together?" Lizzie asked shyly.

"The one we learnt as kids, by the witch fairy." Freddie looked at his sister for confirmation.

Witch fairy? Did he mean Broomhilda? If she'd helped Luna's children, why hadn't she told her? In her excitement, Luna's foot found a loose twig and snapped it as she shifted her weight.

"Who's there?" Freddie spoke sternly, though Luna could feel his heart beating with fear. She slowly stepped out from her hiding place, with her hands in the air.

"Only me. You don't have to be scared of me." The old crone shook, tiny needles of nerves prickling up and down her spine. She couldn't quite believe this was happening, meeting her children, after so many years. Her whole body shook, her energy pouring through every cell in her body. Would she burst? What would happen next?

"I recognise that voice." Lizzie stepped forward. Freddie tried to block her from getting any closer. Luna took another step forward. She couldn't help it, her feet seemed to have a mind of their own. So close to her children, her body propelled itself towards them. Her heart ached to embrace her children, her head a whir of words, thoughts, emotions...Was it a dream? Was the old crone finally going to get to meet her children? Would they remember her?

"Mum? Are you, my mum?" Lizzie asked softly in that voice Luna remembered, that sent good shivers down her spine.

Luna took another step forward, she was so close to Lizzie and Freddie, if she stretched out her hands, she'd be able to touch them. Her fingers shook so badly, she grasped them in front of her. Her body vibrated as if she'd run a marathon. "Yes. Lizzie, Freddie. I am your mother. Are Annie and Katie here too?" Her nails dug into her hands as she stood there, waiting. The silence which lasted a second, seemed an eternity to the old crone.

"Yes, we are here too!" Two women, one blonde and one with dark hair, both wore long ponytails, unmistakeably Luna's other two children, walked through to the front of the crowd. Before Luna could form the next words, Lizzie, Annie, and Katie, flung their arms around her, embracing her in the hug she longed for since the last day she'd set eyes on them. Freddie stepped in to join the family huddled there in the middle of the forest. Luna didn't hear any forest noises, or voices from those gathered, she never wanted the moment to end.

When they released their arms a minute later, Luna noticed the crowd had moved away a little, providing them an amount of privacy for their family reunion. "Why did you leave us?" Freddie asked with a frown. Katie poked him on the arm, but all faces looked at Luna, silently wondering the same question.

The old crone, wrung her hands in front of her, hopping a little from one leg to the next. The question she dreaded, yet so overjoyed to have the opportunity to answer it. "I didn't leave you. I thought I'd be away for a few days. Your dad and your grandparents agreed to look after you. Two weeks later, when I returned, you were gone. There was no trace of you anywhere. I searched and searched for years, in our world, the world you were born in. It broke my heart, losing you. Every day I said a blessing to the goddess to return you to me. I thought your dad and grandparents took you away, maybe changed your names and that you were happy somewhere. My dream for each of you was that you were happy, and safe. I used magic to look for you, and others helped me, using magic to scry to find where you'd gone. I refused to believe you were dead." Luna gulped at the thought, that she'd said that out loud. She wriggled her toes, itchy in her big black boots and thick tights. "Every day, in this realm and the other world, I'd speak to you, as if you were with me, each of you. I dreamt of how you'd look and sound as adults." She stopped, as a horrible thought struck her. "Were you safe, and happy? Were you okay, as children and then adults?" She couldn't bear the answer, but now she'd asked it, she couldn't take it back.

The four siblings looked at each other. It was her oldest daughter who spoke first. "It was so long ago, when we talk about it, we aren't sure if we dreamt our life before we lived here. We remember going to sleep in our beds in a home and waking up in a dormitory of a boarding school. It wasn't bad, and we think a spell was cast so we wouldn't be sad, so we wouldn't remember what we'd lost."

Lizzie put her arm around Annie and continued the story. "We had good friends, and we liked the school, mostly. We learnt some magic, which was fun and a little scary. As teenagers we were taught how to fight, with swords and knives. Freddie's job was to look after the animals, the three of use learnt to cook and sew and make the army uniforms."

"We managed to stay together most of the time. We would talk about where we thought we came from, the time before we could remember." As Katie spoke she reached over and took Freddie's hand. Luna noticed the glances exchanged between the siblings and glimpsed the life they'd led, looking after each other, parents gone, caring for each other, scared, determined, vowing to stay together.

"I'm sorry. That I wasn't there, that I couldn't find you, that I ever left you in the first place." Luna's heart simultaneously breaking and full of joy. She'd found her children and understood keenly what they'd lost. "One night, I learnt I'd magic powers, and my coven called me to help, save the world from evil. It was a fierce war, and as it turned out we didn't succeed. We didn't know that – we thought we'd won. If I could turn back the time, I'd never leave you." She longed to hug each of her children. Did they want to hug her though, the mother who left them?

Freddie stepped close to Luna and hugged her, she felt his love, his forgiveness, his emotions, and his pain. "You had to go and if you are called you would have to do it again. I understand that now. I felt you, every day when you thought of us. I didn't know that was what I felt, but when you said it, it made sense. I longed for something; we all did. Now we know that it was you." He let go of Luna, she thought she'd fall but steadied herself in time. "It will take us a couple of days to make sense of this all, but can we stay with you?"

Without hesitation Luna responded. "Yes. I have a home here and in the modern world and you are all welcome with me, wherever I go. I will go wherever you want to go. I'm not leaving you again, unless want me to."

"What about your coven?" asked Katie. She reached out her hand, her fingers touching Lunas. Sparks flew as the youngest daughter and mother's fingers connected.

"They'll understand. They helped me search for you." Luna responded. Before she could say any of the other words tumbling around in her head, one of the crowd spoke up.

"It's getting dark. We don't want to be in the forest at nightfall. We're going to head to the market town. Are you coming with us?" The man who'd stood near Freddie asked.

Luna spoke loudly enough for the crowd to hear. "The market town should be safe, or you can come with me to Broomhilda's castle, it's protected with Fae enchantments. We'll make sure everyone is safe, fed and has somewhere warm to sleep. Then tomorrow you can head to town or wherever you want to go." As she spoke, she understood this group of adults hadn't had free choice to make any decisions on where to live, eat or sleep, their whole lives.

Chapter Thirty Two

Broomhilda

From her vantage point in her castle, in the room deep underground, Broomhilda kept an eye out for any incidents inside or outside the castle, for miles around the sanctuary. Although she lived in medieval Scotland, her office looked like the incident room at Scotland Yard. Five monitors in front of her showed her the comings and goings across the realm, thanks to Logan's skill with technology.

Using equipment comprising in part modern tech and part witchcraft, the fairy witnessed the dark portal open and swallow the members of the *Mark of the Thirteen*. Another screen showed her Luna surrounded by the crowd of lost children, reunited with her bairns. She crossed her fingers for success for the crone with the reunion; a dozen tiny sparks of light flew from her fingertips. The twinkling lights fluttered up and disappeared as they made their way to Luna, to help light the way.

The screen that revealed the dark cloud changed, flashing an image of Kai, with her friends beside the fire, beside the ruins of The Coven's castle. Relief washed over the oldest fairy – thankful Cain's cousin survived the banishing. She watched as Kai extinguished their fire, and waved her hands, opening a portal, leading the other through it. The castle was going to be full of guests this night. Broomhilda smiled as she felt her castle grew more rooms to accommodate the increased clientele.

Technology having served its purpose. Broomhilda, keen to meet Kai, Stella, Luna and the others as they returned to the castle, left her office and slipped into the tavern. The centre of the castle buzzing, as those who'd stayed prepared and served food and drink to the others, on their return. From her vantage point on the top of the door frame, she could see and hear all the groups gathered around the tables laden with nourishment for those returning from battle, and to accommodate the additional, welcome, guests.

Kai led her group to a table on the edge of the crowd. "I thought you'd appreciate a little quiet, although the tavern is crowded. Please sit while I serve you food and drink. It's the least I can do, after all you've been through." Kai touched Madge's hand, stilling it, knowing her friend's aunt would be itching to serve others. She smiled at Scarlet and her siblings, Sophie and the other servants from Cain's castle, who'd followed her. "Tomorrow is the start of your new life, wherever you wish it to be. Tonight I want to spoil you."

Broomhilda observed the scene in front of her. She'd been ninety nine percent certain Cain's cousin didn't possess an ounce of malevolence, but to see her there, with Madge and the others, relief again flooded through the oldest fairy's body.

The crowd of young people, she'd seen in the forest, released from their slavery, filled Broomhilda with joy and hope for the future. Those who'd returned with Luna mingled with the crowd in the castle. With no evil lurking around the corner, the curse lifted, each young person was intuitively drawn to their family connections. The tavern filled with love as people connected with their clan, deep in conversation with loved ones, who thought they'd been lost forever.

Catherine and Tizzie returned from their clock towers, all thoughts of their adventures faded as they found Luna huddled at a table with her children. Both women hugged Luna, and each of her children in turn. "This is Catherine and Tizzie. My friends, sisters, my coven, who helped me search for you over the last twenty-seven years." Luna touched the hands of each of her children. "Freddie, Annie, Lizzie, and Katie." No need for any words. All the people Luna loved were seated at the table with her.

Broomhilda's energy and enthusiasm grew as she surveyed the scene in front of her. Did she long to be alone? Maybe, and soon enough each group would return to their own homes, and she would make her choice. Tonight was for celebration, for sharing stories, laughing and hugging those who matter.

"I see you hiding up there." Broomhilda smiled at the sound of Stella's voice.

"I'm not hiding, I'm watching as people are reunited with loved ones. Speaking of, where are Maisie and Brigid?" Broomhilda hopped onto Stella's shoulder and slid into one of the pockets of her coat.

"They're checking the people who remained in town are okay. The enchantment shouldn't have impacted them, but Maisie wanted to be sure. They'll be here soon." Stella smiled as she noticed Luna. "Are they...?"

"Yes. Her children." Broomhilda finished the sentence for Stella. "The best outcome, and one we'd wished for, for years. It seems we were successful with ridding the realms of The Coven, and we released everyone who'd been under an enchantment cast by Cain. All the lost children and family members returned."

Stella's energy tingled for Luna, as mother to four children, she understood the pain of regret and being estranged from loved ones. Hot tears of joy for her friend trickled down her cheeks.

"With the curse broken, are you going to your children now?" Broomhilda knew her friend's desire, to reunite with her own children. The oldest fairy one of the council members who voted to keep Stella from her destiny until her children were older, not wanting a repeat of Luna's anguish. The prophecy in the end, came true, though not in the way anyone could have expected.

The Christmas Curse, shared between Luna and Stella, that tore their children away, could it truly be dissolved? Was it too much to ask for? Could she look forward to a happy ending for her and those she loved? Stella wiggled her toes and fingers, lest she burst, the energy building up like the pressure in her ear drums that caused her to yawn. Luna and her children, heads bowed together, as if they'd never been separated. The sight gave her hope. "I've plans to visit my children in a month or so. If we succeeded in banishing Cain. Do we need confirmation of some sort, that we've accomplished it, finally?"

Broomhilda held Stella's gaze. "Cain's gone, his coven with him. Not a threat to us now." She sighed. "As is the way of magic, we don't ever say never."

Before Stella could respond, Maisie and Brigid returned through the portal. Logan, Blair, and Angus right behind them. "Now the party can begin!" Logan called out. The room erupted in hoots of joy, and hand clapping.

Chapter Thirty Three

S tella

Stella, her hands clasped tightly together, pinched the skin of her hand, imperceptibly. She wasn't dreaming, her children were standing in front of her, so close she could touch them. All four of them young adults, all grown up. Pedro, Kay, Emily and Andie. Two olive skinned, two fair, two with freckles, red hair, dark hair, blonde, and sandy coloured – her heart fluttered with joy, and fear. This felt way scarier than facing an evil villain.

Kay, petite, elegant, with her dark hair and perfect skin, dressed in a simple black dress, spoke first. "Hello Mum." She held out her hand. Stella resisted the urge to embrace them all in a hug that lasted forever. Instead, she shook Kay's hand, reluctant to let go, she nevertheless did so, her nerves spiking like a kid stuck with her hand in the cookie jar.

"Hello Kay, Pedro, Andie, Emily. It's so great to see you, all of you." She stood awkwardly, not sure if Andie and Emily would welcome a hug right now or if they wanted to stand back, like the older two. Such an important meeting and turning point in their relationship – she didn't want to do anything wrong. So grateful for her relationship with Emily and Andie, she yearned for a similar connection with the others. While she hadn't seen them for a couple of years, they were still her children, whom she loved bigger than the sky. Now adults with their own lives, and their views of the world. She couldn't take back the past, but hopefully the future meant she could make amends in some way.

Andie and Emily each gave her a quick hug and a peck on the cheek. Both smiled at their mum, sending waves of warmth and love through Stella's heart. The foyer of the hotel where they'd chosen to meet was quiet. Not many people checked in, during the day. The restaurant attached to the hotel stayed open, for travellers, businesspeople, and others to share a cup of tea or a bite to eat. When

Emily suggested they meet at a town in Scotland called Dumfries, Stella booked the first plane she could get to Edinburgh. From there, a train and a bus journey later and she was meeting her children. In the same Scottish market town she frequented in the other realm. Synchronicity. Magic. Hopefully forces working in her favour. The atmosphere the same as the time centuries earlier. The energy of being in Scotland and with her children, maybe dreams can come true.

"I can see why you've always liked Scotland." Andie said, breaking the silence. Her long blonde hair hung in an elegant ponytail. In her cream coloured long pants and shirt she looked all grown up.

"Why is that?" Stella asked, wanting to hug her youngest child, not just for breaking the silence, but that she remembered her stories of a country from so far away. Stories of dragons and witches she'd read as a child, she shared with her children, as bedtime stories.

Andie pointed to the sky outside where clouds tinged with blue danced, playing hide and seek with the sun. "Since we arrived there have been some horrendous storms. Lightning, green and purple clouds. Dark purple." Andie's memory again, Stella's favourite colour – all shades of purple.

"The radio said the anomaly was so unusual, the last time anything like this was seen was nearly thirty years ago. Before that, records dating back into medieval times talk about similar storms." Pedro spoke quietly, seriously, immediately reminding Stella of her son who loved to read, and learn new things, so many years ago. The same sandy hair she remembered ruffling as they played with toy cars on the floor mat. It was shorter now. His grey jeans and blue jumper brought out the colour of his eyes.

"That sounds interesting." Stella said brightly. "Have you seen the northern lights since you've been over here?" She addressed the question to the group, inviting an answer from whomever wished to reply.

"We saw them when we travelled in Europe." Emily smiled. "You'd love it mum. So much old stuff, buildings and nature I mean. I've got lots of photos on my phone. Would you like to come and sit, and I'll show you?" Her beautiful red hair draped loose around her face. Her long emerald dress, embroidered with daisies and leaves perfectly suited her.

"I'd love to." Stella couldn't help the smile spreading across her face. "May I buy you all lunch, if you're happy to sit a while." Terrified of saying the wrong thing, she didn't want the moment to end. She tried to look away as the siblings' exchanged glances.

"Okay." Kay shrugged. "We don't have other plans until later this afternoon."

An hour later Andie's phone rang. "I have to take this." She walked to an empty table chatting quietly to whomever rang her. When she returned Andie leant and hugged Stella. "I'm so sorry Mum, but we have to go. We can meet you for dinner if you're free."

Stella hugged her youngest child. "I'd love that. Text me and I'll come to the restaurant. My treat again. I want to, to spoil you, let you know how much I love you and I appreciate you taking time in your holiday to catch up." She desperately wanted to ask where they were going and if she could join them, but she didn't want to push it. The reunion seemed to be progressing okay so far.

Emily leant and hugged Stella. Her second youngest, and the gentlest soul, with the smile that lit up the room. "I'm glad you came mum." She whispered.

"Me too." Stella replied.

"Thanks for lunch." Kay held out her hand and shook Stella's. Did Stella imagine the warmth as her eldest daughter held her hand for a few seconds longer than before.

"Thank you." Pedro's voice softened a little, or so Stella thought. At least no one ran away, and they were maybe meeting again for dinner. As she watched them leave through the hotel doors, a hundred questions ran around in her head. Where were they going? Sightseeing? She knew they'd hired a car, so who rang them?

An afternoon in modern day Dumfries. Stowing her luggage at reception she booked a taxi. She'd take photos to show Brigid and Maisie what their market town looked like now. She took a deep breath, a huge smile spread across her face. Maybe life could get better, mistakes forgiven, curses lifted, magic working for good, to help and heal. Would she see anyone she recognised in town? Ancestors of those she knew in the other realm. Anticipation, excitement, and energy coursed through her body as she stepped through the door to see what adventures waited for her outside.

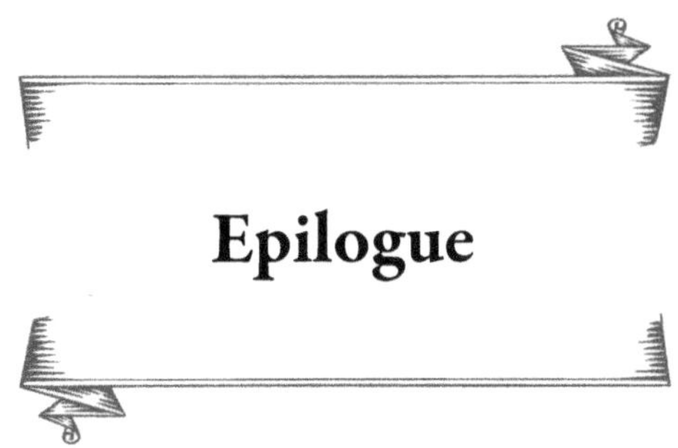

Epilogue

"Oi, you can't sleep there." A man, in his late thirties woke up as another man dressed in an odd uniform prodded him with a stick. He frowned at the train attendant, grabbed his cloak tightly around himself and stood up. The harsh fluorescent light on the ceiling of the train made his eyes sting. He tripped as he stepped off the strange vehicle, his feet landing on the concrete of the underground train station. As he stood, squinting, trying to figure out where he was and more importantly who he was, strangers pushed past. Hurrying on their way home from work, dinner and clandestine romantic twists. He knew none of the ways of these people. He stumbled in the direction of the crowd, exiting the station up a flight of stairs into the sunlight. He blinked; the brightness hurt his eyes. Although he possessed no memory, he knew he wasn't used to this. The heat took his breath, he gasped, breathing in too suddenly, coughs wracked his body.

Why couldn't he remember anything? Nothing in front of him felt familiar, as if he'd never seen any of it before. It's not like he could've been dropped into a brand-new world, that was ridiculous. People pushed and shoved as they strode along the footpath. Headed to where he didn't know. The man cringed, the sharp beeping of a car jarring – such a strange contraption. He raised his hands to his ears, the engine noise of the cars in the street made his ears ache. He took a step back, out of the crowd, finding himself under the awning of a shop. The aroma of coffee, although a scent he couldn't remember, it lured him inside. His stomach crunched – hunger pains cramped his insides. Not a clue when he last ate, or what that meal consisted of.

The café hummed with the sounds of customers enjoying their early lunches, late breakfasts, or morning break, with a cuppa and a taste of whatever pastry they fancied. The walls painted lime and lemon, with a splash of pink and baby blue, the man cared not about the colours, save the fact he wondered why the colours were there.

"What can I get you love?" A lady called from behind a bar filled with sweet smelling foods. The cabinet was cold to touch, while heat emanated from another, that held pockets of pastry. The aromas of the foods fed his hunger, and his confusion.

The man shook his head, not knowing how to answer the woman who stared, waiting for an answer. He wanted to know his name, his location, and why everything felt odd, out of step, out of time. His stomach cried out for food; his parched throat begged him for cooling liquid. He opened his mouth, but no words came out.

"Aren't you hot? In that cloak." She pointed to his cloak, that his fingers were gripping tightly. He looked at his hands and loosened his grip. He shrugged, not knowing what to say, or what to do.

At *Abel's Eatery* none of the customers paid any attention to the dishevelled man, thinking him homeless, or drug addled. Had the owner manned the counter of his establishment, the new café in the middle of the bustling city of Melbourne, alarm bells would have rung throughout the realms. Unfortunately for everyone, the waitress – Mary – feeling sorry for the man, helped him with his cloak, sat him in a corner booth, with a cooked breakfast and a hot tea, and promised to help him.

The End

Sarah Lewin

If you want to know more about me or my books, here are some details. Alternatively, please make contact via any of the social media listed below:

Email: sarahlewin@sarahlewin.com.au

You Tube: https://youtube.com/@sarahlewinangelwisdom539

Blog: https://sarahlewin.com

Facebook: https://www.facebook.com/SarahLewinAuthorWitchyMysteryBooks

Instagram: https://www.instagram.com/sarahlewin_author/

Amazon: https://amazon.com/author/sarahlewin

Goodreads: https://www.goodreads.com/author/show/43342156.Sarah_Lewin

Book Bub: https://www.bookbub.com/authors/sarah-lewin

My Witchy Mystery Books:

<u>Witch Wisdom Series:</u>

#1 – *Crone Wisdom*

#2 – *Ancient Wisdom*

#3 – *The Wisdom of the Witches* (available soon)

There are two free novella's in this series

The Coven

Kai's Story

<u>Spirit Town Cosy Mysteries:</u>

#1 – *Autumn Leaves Are Falling*

#2 – *Secrets Ghosts and Whispers*

<u>I also have a range of children's books available.</u>